THE POACHER'S

Born in Heather Hill on the Cork–Kerry border in February 1939, Cormac MacRua inherits a duty to carry on the tenant rights struggle for which his young father was killed before Cormac was born, and before he could marry Cormac's mother.

When he is six his mother marries his father's half-twin – Brad MacRua, a master poacher. Young Cormac becomes a fascinated and willing apprentice to Brad, and develops a rapport with nature whereby his senses are honed to the cunning of the animals in the wild. At school the MacRua aura sets off a jealous hatred among a few bullies. Cormac devises his own means of survival in the schoolyard jungle. He discovers his sexuality as a relationship develops with two girlfriends who had been school classmates. The confusion of adolescence threatens the values he has so far accepted without question. Only his mother now really understands him, but what he craves is an understanding of his dead father. He experiences the irony of the quatrain:

> *The Law pursues the man or woman*
> *who steals the goose from off the Common,*
> *A greater rascal the Law lets loose,*
> *who steals the common off the goose.*

The greater rascal in this case is Squire Wallace of Highgrove Manor, who owns all the fish, game and hunting rights in the barony. Cormac realises that the killings in the past have failed to provide a solution to this problem. His way of looking to the future finds historical parallel in the emergence of modern Ireland.

At this crucial juncture, Ria, the Squire's daughter, enters the romantic topsy-turvy of his life as he is about to defy tradition and scheme his own way of dealing with Squire.

'Destined to be a masterpiece of literary fiction, this is a story of many dimensions. Aspects of traditional rural Irish life are portrayed with immense clarity and accuracy'

Marilyn Sheehy, *The Kingdom*

'It's a real modern romance, full of lyricism, humour, tension and action . . . a real swashbuckler'

Michael Donovan, *Kerry's Eye*

'Combines poetic description, realistic dialogue and a good "old-fashioned" plot with a positive ending'

Dr Wim Tigges, Professor of Irish Literature, The Hague

First published in 1997 by
Marino Books
An imprint of Mercier Press
16 Hume Street Dublin 2
10 9 8 7 6 5 4 3 2

Trade enquiries to CMD Distribution
55A Spruce Ave Stillorgan Industrial Park
Blackrock County Dublin
Published in the U.S. and Canada by
the Irish American Book Company,
6309 Monarch Park Place, Niwot,
Colorado, 80503.
Telephone (303) 530-1352,
(800) 452-7115.
Fax (303) 530-4488, (800) 401-9705.

© Tommy Frank O'Connor 1997

ISBN 1 86023 050 4

A CIP record for this title is available
from the British Library

Printed in Ireland by ColourBooks,
Baldoyle Industrial Estate, Dublin 13

The Publishers gratefully acknowledge the financial assistance of The Arts Council/An Chomhairle Ealaíon.

THE POACHER'S APPRENTICE

With best wishes

Tommy Frank O'Connor

TOMMY FRANK O'CONNOR

To Sheila and our family

ONE

Seven months after my father was killed I was born into a world of whispering fingers. Fingers pointed at the little MacRua bastard, of a family whose males were born with the instincts of hound and stag. Curling lips whispered about my mother's refusal to stay in her burrow: Deirdre Healy, in love with two men, with my father Cormac, killed before they could marry, and later with Brad, my father's half-twin. In 1945 people recoiled at such behaviour. Deirdre Healy and Brad MacRua let convention go to hell. I was weaned on the wrath of my father's life, on the surging blood of my paternal MacRua ancestors urging vengeance.

I was only six when my mother's marriage to Brad MacRua had me hopping on stepping stones to a new reality. Brad's homestead in the Kerry Glens became home instead of the proud stone house of my mother's people in the more fertile Heather Hill at the other side of the Cork county bounds, over ten miles away. Different houses with their own feeling of home; rosemary, lavender, and bush-roses blend in my scent of boyhood in Heather Hill.

The great stone house at Healy's had a big kitchen between two rooms downstairs and rooms behind a railing upstairs from where I could look down, where the air never tightened.

Before the wedding Brad's house had no stairs, just a square kitchen with a room behind it at the back of the hearth. His mother, my Granny Rua, slept there in a black iron bed with a pattern of creaks telling her every movement behind a bramble curtain that hid the bed from the room. The air in this house stretched between things that happened to family members who were dead and an implied duty on living males to right a growing series of wrongs.

Nibbles of history quickened my boyhood after the wedding: my grandfather, old Brad MacRua, killed in a duel at Highgrove Manor; his daughter, my aunt Ellen, thrown to her death in the flooded Owmore river dividing Highgrove from our Glens; my father, whose name I was given, killed by Squire William Henry Wallace at the manor when seeking to right those wrongs. So much dropping from the roof of history, needing time for Mammy and me to find our place in this new life. I would climb into the purple of the Glens seeking a shade of colour to match my moods, and allow myself to drift back to Heather Hill, to the Healys' way of life before this happened.

Grandma Healy's method of speaking was great: it meant the same thing in Irish or English.

Her tongue couldn't make words: a tangle somewhere in her ears made me learn to speak to her with my face while she taught my hands to make meanings with signs. It was fun: I could speak two languages two ways, just like Mammy.

'You might have to go to school in the Kerry Glens and that might turn your living upside down,' was what came straight from her heart as the wedding day drew closer. 'But don't ever forget that you can be at home here any time you want, as long as it's all right with your mother.'

'What about Brad?' I asked.

Her hands had tried to sign something different from what was in her eyes, before gathering me to her. She pressed my head to her chest, the thumping of her heart under the vibrations of a sigh, not wanting to let me go. Protecting me, from what? While she cleaned her glasses on the tail of my shirt I tossed a worry into her woe.

'The priest here made Mammy cry just like you now; I hate anyone that makes my Mammy cry. Brad wouldn't let him do it, I know he wouldn't because he pulled the shillelagh off that priest in the Glens that shouted at him.'

She turned me around to face her eyes. 'He pulled the shillelagh off a priest! Where was Granny Rua?'

'She was looking for me outside; she didn't know I had stolen back in through the bedroom window.'

'Oh Mother of God, who is my gentle Deirdre making her life with; he didn't hit the priest, surely?'

'No; but the priest wilted when Brad broke the blackthorn and threw it on the fire.'

'The priest, what did he say? Did he – curse?' She held her face and waited with matching mouth and eyes.

'Sure that would be a sin. No, he didn't curse; he just listened. Well, he had to listen because Brad took a grip on his coat and asked him what he knew about honour.'

'Oh Mother of God!' Sometimes her face said everything; no need to watch her hands.

'But he didn't hit the priest; he just gripped him tight, like uncle Danny holding the big hammer.'

'But the priest was frightened, terrified surely, young Cormac, even if he deserved it?'

'Well, he was shouting something about my father and Brad and Mammy that I couldn't understand. That's when Brad broke the blackthorn in front of his face.'

'Can you remember what you couldn't understand?'

'Something about the Bible and about a brother taking his brother's wife. That priest didn't want Brad to marry Mammy, just like the one here didn't want Mammy to marry Brad. But they want to marry each other; I know they do.'

'So you stole away from Granny Rua again to listen to Brad and our Deirdre?'

'No. They were in the kitchen. I could hear they were happy with each other, in between Granny Rua's snores.'

'You're a terrible case, young Cormac, a terrible case.' She always cuddled me to her when she said that.

The men had to convert their talk into stones and mortar by building a room at the lower end of Brad's house before the wedding.

Granny Rua came to stay with Granma Healy, while Granpa and uncle Peter moved to the Glens with Mammy. Peter, her eldest brother, was a bachelor. He had Granma Healy's placid looks, looked a bit like Mammy, tall and lean with sandy hair. Sometimes you couldn't see his face under the hat he always wore outdoors. A special slot in his teeth held a turned-down pipe that seemed as natural a part of him as his nose. People remarked that the level or plumbline that disagreed with Peter's eye should be double-checked before it was followed. He had learned the stonemason's trade from Granpa Healy, who was always found opposite Peter as stone walls rose to become houses at both sides of the county bounds.

In Heather Hill I voiced Granma Healy's signs as my grandmothers talked over the years since they last met. My wonder soaked up aspects of their chat, such as Granma Healy's manœuvring, like a chicken trying to lay her first egg, to sign a question for Granny Rua about her men's friendship with danger. Her eyes couldn't hide that sense of danger playing hide-and-seek in the

Glens. Granny Rua straightened herself in the chair and remarked on how calm life in Cork seemed to be in contrast with the hazards in the Glens of Kerry.

Glens men worthy of the name were expected to face danger when honour and the welfare of their families dictated it. A persecuted community expected more of some men than of others. The MacRuas, feared faction fighters in the last century, were known as men who would not lie down under oppression.

They were the men who had asked questions about unfair laws supporting the dynasty of Highgrove Manor on the clovery lap of Hare Mountain across the Owmore river from the rugged Glens.

Granma Healy grew agitated. She wanted to sign something to Granny Rua through me, but her fingers worried as if unravelling a tangle.

'You say tradition is being passed on, and that is good. But I see the mantle of danger being handed on too, each generation embroidering their crimson craft on it. Things have changed. Surely, with the new squire at the manor, all those old sores can be allowed to heal.'

She steadied her head in her hands, then patted her hair before going on. 'Young Cormac's dad – he was a daredevil; he must have been a terrible worry to you? And it was that aura about him that lured my Deirdre. What she saw in him made me so fearful, and the same thing is dancing now between Brad and herself. More danger, Niamh MacRua. Does he have to obey the hazards of his tradition? Can't he leave the past rest with the dead? Wouldn't he obey you, if you asked him as a mother, if you were to advise him that his hurry could hasten him to his place among the dead before his time, like his twin?'

I was there linking their thoughts but I was no longer noticed, no more than Granny Rua noticed her tongue or Granma Healy noticed her hands. Granny Rua wove the thoughts of her heart in her native Irish, as in the bedtime stories she told me in the Glens.

I drift into the yard on the warmth of a sunny day, hens cackling at the findings of their scratchings, calling their chicks to share the prize. Then a shadow hovers in their world, will not be scratched away: hens calling, chicks gathering, hawk diving, feathers floating, falling, rising. I jump on a cock's feather and chase after the hawk.

When I awoke, Granny Rua was speaking as if whispering to angels. 'I should have been shy but he made me feel we had known each other all our lives. He took my hand into the vigour of his. Somewhere inside me a lark soared into the heavens. In that moment I became his for ever.'

I could see by the sparkle in her eyes that she was telling her story about my dead grandad when he had been young like Brad. Granma Healy seemed to understand what she was saying. I resumed my signing, and learned more about the people in the MacRua family.

'"I'll be up at Tureen lake very early Sunday, even before cockcrow. You mustn't tell anyone but if you're up and out that early, I'd like to meet you again," he said.

'He must have known that I could have been tortured and wouldn't have whispered a word. He had trusted me, honoured me with a secret.

'I was there when cockcrow woke up the day but there was no sign of him. Maybe I was at the wrong part of the lake, I thought. It must have been over two miles around. He could have been anywhere. Then out of the ferns at the water's edge he rose and came to me.

'He was wet but his clothes were dry. He had been doing something in the lake. I didn't ask; I knew he wouldn't tell me.

The cold shivered on him. I put my hands to his face and kissed him. It lit up his eyes, so I kissed him again. He drove his fingers into my long brown hair and whispered my name as if he was caressing every syllable: "Niamh; Niamh Brosnan!" Then he tensed, hands to my shoulders. His eyes caught something behind me in the trees. A puck and four goats stood and waited. He moved up to them. They pointed their snouts towards him without fear, as if he were one of their own. Next thing he squatted among them, selected one and felt her udder. He squeezed her teats into his hand and tasted the milk. Then he lay down and brought her udder over his mouth and took some of her milk. It was pure natural the way he did it. For anybody else it would have been mad.

'He beckoned me to him. I was afraid the goats would run. He settled them with his eyes so I stole up, trying to be like him. He eased me back with him, and moved the two teats of that wild goat over my blushing face. I opened my mouth and tasted the warm herby milk. Then with one hand under my head he brought my lips to her teat. Again he squeezed: some of the milk spattered on my face. I felt so safe in his wild world.

'After he sent the goats on their way I found myself lying on the ground, with him propped on his elbow alongside. He drew me to him and nibbled the milk off my face. He saw some briar scratches below my hemline that I hadn't even noticed.

'What did he do but select some herbs and chew them up, settling me with his eyes. He gripped my knee in one hand and then licked the mess all over my briar scratches. You can imagine the feelings shooting through me, Mary Healy! I was his prisoner and he didn't seem to know it. It was only the scratches he was licking but he was sending feelings from my toes right up to where his fingers had searched my hair.'

Granma Healy was helping my translations with her own hands. I wondered if Brad ever did funny things like that with Mammy. So many things about Granny Rua's Brad matched up with my uncle Brad. Again I signed her words.

'He stood up, keeping my hand with him, and whipped me on to my feet with that fast arm of his. The birds began their morning chorus to add to my thrill of being close to him. He whispered how we would next meet. I squeezed myself against him to agree. The fact that I had to ask my mother first was only a little mountain to climb.'

'And how did you do that?' I asked for Granma and me.

'Through my father. I won his agreement first. I could see he was worried but something in his eyes and the start of a smile when I assured him I'd be fine, settled the worry. My mother? Well, she was worried too but she could see that I was gone anyway.

'"At least you'll never go hungry while you're with him," she said, "and a MacRua never wronged a woman. But you'll have many a long night when neither you nor anyone else will know where he is or what he's up to. Oh, it'll be something dangerous in the wild.

'"You've listened like me to stories of what Brad MacRua attempts under the cover of darkness. Water bailiffs and civic guards try to match his wits, and you won't know if he has outwitted them again until he's back in your bed before dawn. And even then you'll not be any the wiser where he has been or how close he has come to something terrible."

'My sister wondered if there were any more fish like that in the lake. My brothers laughed and said that Brad MacRua, who could have a mermaid out of the sea if he wanted one, was hardly likely to settle for an article like me that would forget where I was in the middle of my jobs if I took a fit of singing!'

Then she slowed down and closed her eyes. 'The first time I saw him indoors was when he came to our house to ask my father and mother for me to be his wife. I could see he was as much at home in a house as a stag in a byre. My brothers were quieter than I had ever seen them. My sister thought it wasn't fair, she having the looks and I having the luck, and surely there must be someone else like him in the Glens. My father did his best to make him feel at home. It wasn't that he was distant; my Brad could talk about anything from the price of cattle to new and old wars. My mother fell in love with him. She said that he would sometimes break my heart but that the good times would be out of this world.'

She paused as we rearranged ourselves in our chairs. 'So I can understand, Mary Healy, how your Deirdre found her heart straining to be one with my Cormac's, and now Brad's. She had to follow that lure. Deirdre is a beautiful girl, a lady by nature just like you. I'm sure she'll live some of her dreams with her Brad, just as I did with mine. Only I hope he won't be taken from her like mine was.'

Granny Rua spoke of women's danger too, of how she would have loved to have a daughter to fill the place of Ellen who had been drowned, but her childbearing had ended with that almost fatal effort to have her twins.

Granma Healy told of her pride and joy in Deirdre, a gift born seven years after Danny, the younger of her two sons. I found it hard to imagine uncle Danny Healy, the blacksmith in Knockeen Village forge, as a boy. To me at the time he seemed enormous, just about tall enough to look over the back of a horse but almost as broad as that same animal, his brown curls bulging in a sooty black cap; fire in his eyes, sometimes warm, sometimes scorching.

Granma Healy worried that neither Danny nor Peter had made any move towards building a family of their own.

'Now that Deirdre is to settle into a normal married life, one of them might make a move,' Granny Rua said.

I found myself being drawn into the plaintive look in Granma Healy's eyes. 'God knows a house needs children in every generation,' she said. She teased my hair again. This time I went into the safe world of her arms and swam into the sleep that closed my eyes.

I saw another side to my mother the day she took me to Millstreet to fit me out for the wedding. Her previous efforts to get me into footwear had failed after I left the first pair in Brad's piggery to see what would happen. I got Danny's greyhounds to fight over the next ones, a pair of sandals. The greyhounds chewed them up.

The day got off to a bad start when she found her brothers had forgotten to have the wheels of her cart reshod, so she couldn't take it on the road.

'Always the same,' she muttered. 'The tailor won't mend his own trousers; the blacksmith won't shoe his own wheels.'

Peter and Danny suggested that she could borrow a cart but were sorry they said anything. That morning she ignored Grandma's protesting hands as she removed the pony's tackling and put on the saddle. I hadn't known up to then that a saddle was for a man. Mammy mustn't have known at all because she hoisted me up in front of it and threw me her bags to hold. Then she dug her foot in the stirrup and swung herself over the saddle. She tucked me into position in front of her as we trotted off, leaving Granma Healy taking turns at blessing herself and holding her head. Tucked in front of her there in the saddle it was as if the pony adjusted her trotting to Mammy's own movements.

New magic in this closeness, even better than when I snuggled into her warmth in bed. She filled our journey with talk about the new outfit she was getting me for the wedding and how after it was over I would have a real father in Brad. A firmness in her voice made me happy because I knew she was sure about everything.

Mr Lyons in the doorway of his shop regarded us with curiosity as Mammy drew up the pony and hitched her to the railings. Two heads inside the window also found us more interesting than whatever they were supposed to be doing but when we went into the shop we found that we were the only customers. One of the girls looked like a cleaned-up older version of Snotty Higgins, the ugly creature from the class ahead of me at school who used to pester me with nasty comments about having no father, until I wrapped her a present of a dead rat from Brad's piggery. She took more care of her words after that.

My instincts were soon proved right when Snotty's lookalike took a fit of giggling after Mammy produced a pair of stockings Granma Healy had knitted and asked me to put them on. The other assistant and fat Mr Lyons also seemed to find the incident amusing. Mammy didn't.

A redness blushed through her neck into her face, just like when the priest tried to block her plans to marry Brad.

With one mind we removed the stockings and took ourselves diagonally across the street to Hogan's where I reluctantly settled for a sturdy pair of black boots costing almost two shillings. Mammy didn't buy any clothes for herself because her aunt had sent on the full wedding rigout from Boston before she almost married my father. She left a list in two shops to be collected another time by her brothers to cater for extra visitors to the house for the wedding.

At the wedding, uncle Danny was too big for his suit. His head looked smaller since Brad tidied up his hair with the sheep shears. Mammy plastered my hair with a mixture of honey and warm water. It felt like a cap.

'Th'old cap will fit you now, Uncle Danny,' I whispered, as Granma Healy stood me in the seat beside him. Everybody laughed. Someone behind me tossed my hair. Brad winked across at me from the other side of the aisle.

He held his finger to his lips for me to keep quiet but the glint in his eye said he didn't mean it.

The Canon was rigged out in his full gear on the altar. He didn't smile, not used to the early hour, I supposed. He looked at me as if a pig had pissed in his chalice. Two fiddlers played a light march. I looked back to see Mammy stepping up the aisle on Granpa's left arm. He looked grand, like a Pharaoh. Even the sun came up to have a look at Mammy and the happy proud way she carried herself. Brad took Granpa's place alongside her. He looked happy. Brad's cousin Breda stood at our side of Mammy and uncle Peter didn't seem happy without his hat and pipe over at the far side of Brad.

The Canon rattled away in Latin and the clerk threw some of it back to him for a while, before coming to the front of the altar and asking Brad something like:

'Do you, Carraig MacRua, take this woman . . . ?'

Granpa was at the outside of the seat so I leaned past Granma Healy to tell him that the Canon had made a mistake. My Mammy was marrying Brad; the sour sleepy Canon had called him 'Carraig'. Uncle Danny pulled me back into my place and told me to stop myself.

'It mightn't look it,' he said, 'but the Canon served his time; he knows what he's at.'

Brad said 'I do.'

The Canon then asked the same question of Mammy. He

18

stopped and glared at me after saying her name 'Deirdre Healy', and then continued after I nodded that he got it right this time. Mammy said, 'I do.' I was delighted. I gave Danny a puck of my elbow. His looked like he had spent a good day shoeing cartwheels, only his face was cleaner.

I looked at Granma Healy; she was crying. I looked at Granny Rua – the same. On my word, I took a good look around me and all the women were at it: dabbing hankies and taking them away as if afraid they might be seen. Some of the men looked a bit shifty too, but they all managed to blink or sniff it away, and smile.

I prayed to God that Mammy or Brad wouldn't turn around and see the weeping and sniffling of the crowd of *óinseacha* behind them.

That all changed after we got back to the festivities at Healy's house. Two tables were joined together in the lower room and softened with a sheet under lovely white tablecloths. Mammy and Brad had to sit at one side of the Canon, and cousin Breda and uncle Peter at the other. Everyone was glad when sourpuss left with a mixture of goat, goose and pig in his belly, washed down with the start of the amber bottle. Uncle Danny escaped from his jacket and tie and when the Canon's horse and trap crossed the bridge to head down to Knockeen it was like the teacher opening the door for playtime at school.

Granpa gave a speech and said that now that Mammy was leaving Heather Hill there was a gap for another woman to fill. He hoped that between his two sons the delay wouldn't be too long. The crowd picked this up and sent suggestions buzzing around my uncles. Danny beat at them as if they were a swarm of wasps and remembered he had to go looking for something. Peter just smiled and puffed away on his pipe.

After Uncle Danny drove Mammy and Brad to the train to go away for a few days, things slowed down as the sun settled in for a direct overhead view. Granpa took what was left of the goat and the piglet from the roasting spits in the yard and brought them inside where Granny Rua trimmed them on to the muslin for Granma Healy and Breda to spice. Peter was still making no shape to search for a woman to replace Mammy. Someone had to do something about it, so I put it to Breda that she could fill the gap like Granpa had asked in his speech.

I hadn't noticed while I was absorbed in what their deft hands were doing to the meat that it was all women in the kitchen and the men were gathered in the yard. My proposition to Breda raised a gaggle of laughter. Her hands hid the soft brown windows in her face.

'I'll kill you, young Cormac,' she said; but she only grabbed and hugged me. She was blushing and laughing. Granma Healy joined in the hilarity while tossing my hair with her herby greasy hands. Granpa came in to remove the carcasses but he wanted to share in the fun too. Before you could say 'wedding ring' Peter was presented before me to hear a repeat of what I had originally intended as a helpful proposition to Breda. Peter didn't let me down. He asked Breda to join him for a polka just starting on the flagstones out in the yard. Breda took off her apron and wiped her hands. Granma did the same and danced with Granpa.

My wedding boots and myself were just getting used to each other by the time Mammy arrived back with Brad a few nights after the wedding. Granny Rua had settled herself in the old room. I was about to climb into the new smells of the new bed in the new room when I heard a tackled horse trotting into the yard.

My excitement at their return landed like a stone in my stomach when I found they had made further adjustments to sleeping arrangements. I would have to sleep on a new feather tick at the back of the hearth in Granny Rua's room and Brad would join Mammy in the new bed. Reading the disappointment in my face, they promised that I could move to the loft over the new room when that was finished. Though Mammy looked happy with the new arrangements I knew that a few nights of Brad's elbows and knees, and talking in his sleep without even knowing what he was saying, would change her mind.

Meanwhile I would have to forget about snuggles in bed because the dip in the middle of Granny Rua's seemed to be just the right size for her. And my bed was different. Something else missing: yes, the scent of rosemary from the bed clothes; no rosemary bushes in the Glens. I remembered Granma Healy's offer and spent most of that summer in Heather Hill.

Granpa Healy tamed my anger by showing me how to dress stones for building, getting to know the stone and preparing it for its place with hammer and cold chisel. He had a way of coaxing me into proud stories of how craft and skill in stone brought out the best in people the world over. I would watch as Peter or himself twisted and turned a stone to find how best it would lie in a wall. If it was too awkward they would smarten it up with a few hammer strokes: suddenly that stone would find the slot designed for it alone.

Then the next stone would become the most important in the world until dressed to face the elements and settled into its own special bed. I watched as stones were picked up and thrown aside all day and wondered if they were disappointed. Then in the evening I was glad when they would show a face that would win them their intended place, alive in powerful walls.

When I first saw drawings of the pyramids I was sure Granpa

21

and his father had built them. It never occurred to me that he wasn't there with the Egyptians dressing those mighty chunks of rock into shape before rolling and levering them into place. Sometimes I would lose his words, enthralled by the eloquence of his face, that smile dancing into a laugh, his bushy eyebrows stroking wonder into those pictures and the tawny moustache twitching as he studied me between sentences.

Some days I brought dinner in two tin gallons to uncle Danny and Leftie, his helper, in the forge. One gallon contained milk, the other a stew of bacon or mutton, rabbit caught by Danny himself, and potatoes, herbs and vegetables from Granpa's garden. That garden missed Mammy's hand just like I did, and there was a roughness about uncle Danny I hadn't noticed before Mammy got married.

Granpa warned me not to go near Danny's forge on wet mornings because of fear of thunder and lightning but he said it in whispers away from Danny's hearing. Sometimes the thunder came home from the forge with him and after clattering around the house he would take it out into the fields. Maybe Uncle Danny frightened all the danger off to the Glens.

Then Granpa would look at Granma and say, 'Someone would want to be making a move around here, and soon.'

Uncle Peter would just puff on his pipe and pretend not to hear.

Two

Scents of the Glens on my return from Heather Hill: musk of hay and oats straw soften the tang of pig from the manure heap. Mixture of peat and bracken swirl in blue smoke in the September air. Brad has trained his dog, Loopy, to keep the gander in check. A section of the haggard, permanently ploughed by sows, is fenced off as a kitchen garden. Yes, my new home.

Just one field away from the back of our house a forest ran from the Owmore river, in the valley separating us from Hare Mountain, right up to the top of the Glens. Could this be where danger played hide-and-seek, I wondered. Ash, oak, sycamore, birch and palm climbed over clusters of bushy undergrowth. Hare Mountain on the other side looked even more fertile than Heather Hill where Mammy and I had lived. It sat there opposite us, fat and green, from the cliff over the river, through the wide slopes, and seemed to have borrowed a piece of our Glens to make a purple cap for its head. I couldn't imagine danger as being fat; it had to be wild.

Nearly everyone in the school was barefooted like myself. I was put sitting beside a girl called Betsy Foran because all the other seats in first class were full. She might just as well have been called Snotty Foran. Betsy didn't sniffle so much but glazed the stuff across her cheeks with her cuffs.

Hurling wasn't allowed in the school grounds; football could be played only on the ground in the tight field sloping away from the back of the schoolyard. We didn't have a football at first but Brad solved that by compressing strong heather with horsehair and feathers into a ball held together in tight sacking.

That Christmas Santa Claus made a mistake and left presents in both my homes, a hurley in Heather Hill and a book about living creatures and their habits in the Glens. Brad introduced me to his world of the night, the same places but with a more tingling feeling than the day. Frost hardened the fluffy snow into a crisp whiteness, fitting an edge to the background stillness. He took me to a different part of the forest, each night further up among the rowan trees. With my eyes closed I learned to concentrate on the sounds made by wind and water, by the birds and animals of the night.

I wondered at the discipline, rhythm and pattern of those sounds, and the way Brad could select one out of all the others, reproduce it himself and explain what was making it in which part of the forest. Almost every sound had a purpose, I learned; it was looking for a response or responding to another sound or a mating call. Anything not in harmony with that natural order was to be regarded with caution.

That knowledge gave me a thirst for more as I sought a step-by-step mastery of the layers in the chorus of the night. The more in tune my ear became, the more I realised I had to learn. The more I wanted to learn, the keener Brad would lay out ways to train my senses.

He explained how owls and bats guided their flight by rebounding sound; an instinctive echo-system. Yet the owl could surprise a rat or fieldmouse with a fifty-foot swoop. He led me into the wonder of the keen senses of animals such as dogs and deer; into their ability to pick up a sound or scent at long distances. Later, he promised, he would awaken my sense of smell.

One night after we ate our supper of milk, brown bread and

salmon, he showed me how my developing ear could be used. Mammy went to bed early because she needed the rest. She had a baby in her belly from sleeping with Brad since the wedding. Brad took a square of bread. We broke it into about eight pieces and daubed it with goose grease before putting it in a skin sack inside his coat.

'Tonight,' he whispered, 'we'll move towards the river.' Something sparkled in his eye. Again there were the common sounds, some louder, with more of an edge than others. The waters in the gorge that ran towards the river rippled where further upstream they babbled. The whispers from the river were difficult to separate from the breeze in the trees. That was one of the exercises Brad had given me. He was hearing sounds my ear still couldn't separate but he soothed my impatience by reminding me of how much I had already learned.

I was just about to remark on the noise of prowling dogs when Brad coaxed them into view. He fed each one a piece of bread and encouraged me to pat them as he did. Another piece for each of them and the terrier became my friend immediately.

The German shepherd still growled at me so Brad gripped his neck just behind his ears and got me to rub my hair to the dog's nose. It worked. He stopped growling at me. Then, with a tighter version of the mouth noises he was teaching me, he sent the dogs away, and guided me through the undergrowth to a cluster of furze bushes. The hairs stood on the back of my neck. He bade me to remain perfectly still and listen. Observing him there crouched within the bushes was like watching a cat waiting for the mouse it knew would come. He wasn't just listening; he was poised, sometimes with eyes closed. Still not a word about danger.

In the near distance behind us a noise fractured the night. The crack of a twig on the floor of the forest signalled the stealthy sounds of human feet and the whispered controlling of the dogs. Brad pointed to his nose as the sounds stole closer and closer still to a sycamore whose branches reached over our vigil. I dared not turn around to see whom Brad was watching as they paused behind me. Yes; this was it. This was real.

From where they stood they could see over a mile of Owmore river working its way through Benmore valley. They could see Hare Mountain looking like a sleeping giant in the night, bathing his feet in the river. In the middle of his large apron he hid Highgrove Manor among oak, sycamore, beech and fir soldiers, but in a way that allowed Highgrove to watch us.

The men searched the night with powerful lights wired to batteries on their backs. Pigeons, rooks, jackdaws, magpies and owls cackled from their roosts overhead. The dogs rose a hare between us and the river but the hare turned them and sped off into the safety of the upper Glens, taking the dogs and the night searchers after him. Still Brad didn't move, crouching there while the night settled things back into their places. The barking of the dogs had faded into the upper Glens when he took me by the hand. We crept back up the forest and along by the lower shelter of the ditch through the field to our house.

Instead of going in the door he took me around to the back of the house and put me in through the kitchen window. He suggested that I go to sleep with Mammy and if she awoke to tell her everything would be fine. I waited until he mingled with the night. Granny Rua's old bed creaked without the accompaniment of her snoring, so I crept into the room to find out why.

'Ah, young Cormac, ye're back, thanks be to God.'

'You sound a bit worn out, Granny.'

'Indeed; worn out. That's what it is, I suppose.' She handed me a ponny. 'Half-fill that out of the kettle and splash a drop of goat's milk in it for me, like a good boy.'

She needn't have asked. Whenever the night troubled her the mixture of warm water and goat's milk and a drop from her own special bottle was sure to stretch her in the bed.

I crept in beside Mammy in the new bed. 'Ah it's yourself, Cormac; where's Brad?'

'He brought me home and went off again. He said to tell you everything will be fine.'

'I hope he's right, my little man; I hope he's right. Snuggle into me here now and we'll have a big sleep.'

I purred in my closeness to her without daytime things pulling her away from me. And then she spoilt everything. 'Would you like a little sister, young Cormac?'

I pretended not to hear. A little sister! There were lots of questions I wanted to ask Mammy or Brad, or the two of them together. Everywhere I turned there were tiny little baby clothes being knitted. Even Granma Healy in Heather Hill was at it, the thread of worn jumpers taking on new life in her hands.

And then there was this question of the shape Mammy was in. The new Snotty Higgins was lurking in Mammy's swollen tummy. I had a good idea of how she got in there but wondered when and how she would come out and make my life a misery. Was it like a calf coming out of a cow, or a lamb coming out of a sheep? Mammy took me and my worries into the haven of her cuddles. In the morning Brad followed a teasing aroma into the bright room to coax me out of the bed from which Mammy had crept without me even noticing.

That breakfast of oatmeal, potato cake and salmon steak was the tastiest in ages. The contentment in the house, the serenity around Mammy and Granny and Brad quenched the questions that were bothering me.

In the dairy after breakfast Brad's eye was firmly on mine as he introduced me to a whole cock salmon.

'How d'you know it's a cock; there's no red comb on his head, like a rooster?'

'That spike there in the front of his mouth; that's what makes him different from the hen. There are other differences too, ones you'll learn to feel later when they're alive in the water.'

'In the water! You can feel the fish while they're still in the water?'

'That's for another time, young Cormac.'

'But how can you tell the difference between a cock and a hen under the water? Would the cock pick at you like a red rooster?' Even dead, he had a fierce look about him.

'No, you must wait and learn; the nearest I can get is that the hen is more playful, like Ginger.'

'Ginger, our cat?'

'You know when you rub her, she kind of fits herself into your hand and doesn't want you to stop. There's a feel to the hen salmon a bit like that.' His left hand moved with the words.

'So why can't you take her out of the water like you did with the cock?'

'Because she lays the eggs, and the smolts hatch out of them like chicks or goslings out of our farm eggs or like tadpoles out of the frog spawn down in the swamp on your way to school.'

'But after she hatches the eggs?'

'She doesn't hatch them. She lays them in a soft sandy spot in the ford of the river and covers them. After that she's out of season and has other work to do in the natural order of things.'

I was going on eight when I received first communion in Benmore church. I was ready for more information but Brad wasn't always ready for my questions.

'Can I ride Stepper again today, Uncle Brad? I can trot with her now no bother.'

Stepper was our sturdy young pony and she could move about the steep faces of the Glens almost as well as our Kerry cows, and she was so strong.

'Yes, you can get to know Stepper. She'll not harm you if you talk to her and walk her gently.'

The excitement of the wonders Brad was feeding to my hungry mind and the adventure of being with Stepper made me forget to talk to him about my own troubles. Things were becoming very strange with Mammy. Whenever I set up a chance to talk with her Brad would be there too, and I couldn't fit my questions between their togetherness. To add to my worries, Granny's snoring was more interrupted and irregular as nights went on.

Stepper was only half my age, and, even though she couldn't answer me, I wondered aloud to her about this sister that was coming to torment us. I worried if Mammy would be all right after the snotty creature crawled out of her stomach. I wondered why Brad would hold Mammy against him and whisper things to her that I couldn't hear. What, I secretly worried, if Granny Rua's breathing didn't settle into a snore after the boiled water and goat's milk with a little drop of the clear stuff from the bottle under the tick?

Our dog Loopy tagged along everywhere Stepper and I went, unless Brad ordered him to stay. Even though he was only two years old it was amazing how clever he was. A word or a whistle from Brad would always get the same reaction from Loopy; gathering the cattle, bringing back a stick or potato which Brad or I had thrown or just sitting or lying down.

At Hallowe'en time that year I explored among the bushes at

the Hare Mountain side of Owmore river. I told myself I was looking for witches and ghosts but I deliberately selected the cliff from where Aunt Ellen was thrown to her death, hoping to meet her ghost. There in the bushes and rhododendron I saw what looked very like a pair of wheels.

'You've the eye of a falcon, just like your grandfather,' Brad said as we prepared to recover my apparently precious find. I put the tackling on Stepper while Brad gathered every piece of rope and chain in the place. Even Loopy was allowed to come along as dusk took the odd look off our mission.

After a survey of the scene Brad established that it was indeed an old black trap that was no longer up to standard for Highgrove. He unwedged and gradually lowered it to our bank, using Stepper to keep the ropes tight, before making his own thorny way down to us.

'If they dumped it there they won't mind us having it?'

'They'd resent it being of use to anyone else, and especially to us.'

'Why us, Brad?'

'Because our family and them have different ways of looking at things.'

'Something about their eyes, is it?'

He gave me a funny look.

'In a way, yes: they see themselves as more important; above us in their own minds. And that squire owns every fish that swims in the rivers, every deer and hare, every fox and badger, every pheasant and grouse and woodcock; and if he turns out like his father he'll think he owns the people as well.'

'What about the two salmon you caught that late night?'

'That's a MacRua secret, our family heritage.'

'Family heritage – to steal salmon?'

He urged me to keep my voice down, explaining that sound bounces off the water in the river. 'Not stealing: taking what's rightfully ours. I'll explain to you when you're older. Your father would want me to do that.'

'So that's why they wouldn't want us to st . . . take this old trap?'

'That and the fact that they depend on us for their fun and games.'

'Fun and games?' I tried to imagine what kind of a game the squire and Brad could play together. It couldn't be football or hurling; definitely not catching fish.

'You'll soon learn: when there's a banquet or a hunt ball coming up, we'll be sent for to kill and cure their game and to act as ghillies for the hunt, or for shooting or fishing.'

There was a bother inside him, like something waiting for the right pattern of words.

'They must like us so, when they ask our help?'

'The Wallaces like the MacRuas! God help your innocence! As they see it that's our place, to help them.'

'Did that make my dad angry too?'

'He liked the hunt. The attitude of some hunters maddened him, like when they galloped over people's crops in the fields: the same as galloping over the people, he always thought.'

'Did they ever gallop over ours?'

'Once too often, and found their hunt dogs dead next morning.' He seemed happier now, working on the trap.

'Won't they know this trap when they see it; 'tis pure black.'

''Twon't be pure black when they see it.'

Brad had Stepper tackled to the trap when he woke me in the middle of the night. I was to make it lively to Nurse Relihan, who was expecting to be called anyway for Mammy but Granny Rua needed her too for a different reason. When we stopped at her house it was wrapped in stillness. I'm not sure what the time was but the only other life moving was on wings.

When she woke up to the meaning of my message she threw a leather bag to me, pulled a coat over her nightclothes and ran, her shawl dragging along the ground. Stepper cut out a fast pace on the return while Nurse grumbled the cold out of herself in the shawl.

Stepper stopped at the gate even though it was open. Nurse released a hand from the shawl and blessed herself. 'The Lord have mercy on the dead,' she said.

I got out and went to Stepper's head to guide her through the gate but it was as if she was waiting for a train to pass. 'The Lord have mercy on your innocent soul,' Nurse said but she wasn't looking at me. It was as if she was speaking to whatever was stopping Stepper from going through the gateway. Then I remembered Brad telling me about a barn fire at Highgrove Manor during the Black and Tan war and how the horses had been led through the fire with their heads covered. I thought about borrowing nurse's shawl, but then Stepper moved, so I jumped into the trap and a minute later despatched a silent nurse at the door.

Brad waited. This time he sent me for the priest. Granny Rua had passed away only a few minutes earlier.

I would have to rush. Then I understood why Stepper had stopped at the gate. I had heard that the spirit sometimes does a tour of its own place after leaving the body and that only horses can see it. So Stepper waited until Granny Rua had passed by our gate. This just wasn't fair, I kept telling Stepper.

Granny Rua, even though she snored and woke me at night,

was just the right kind of a granny for our house. Now she was gone, and what were we getting instead? Another Snotty Higgins! Father Dwyer was awake anyway and said he'd ride ahead on his own saddled horse.

'But you've been crying, *a mhic*?'

'I told you, Father, my Granny Rua's dead. If you had a Granny Rua and she died, you'd be crying too.'

I gave Stepper her head back the way we had come. She slowed at the gate but trotted through it up home. On my left the sun was brightening up the place it would rise from to bring me this new and terrible day.

No one waited in the yard or at the door. I didn't want to see anybody except Granny Rua. I untackled Stepper. She seemed to understand the way Granny Rua and the new Snotty swapped positions in my head. I dragged myself through the front door to hear Mammy and the nurse shouting at each other in the new room. Brad was tipping a pot of boiling water into the zinc bath in the kitchen. Mammy would have done it a lot smarter.

'Tell that snappy old nurse she can leg it home on her own if she does anything to Mammy.'

Brad looked up and half tried to stop me from going up to Granny Rua's bed.

Fr Dwyer and Lily Mack were saying prayers at each other across the bed which had now been pulled out from the wall. The old bramble curtain was gone and the walls had been freshly whitewashed. I stood looking at Granny Rua's face, the colour matching the lime on the walls.

It was her face all right but it had stopped. It had stopped struggling for breath. Shuttered eyes stilled under lids frozen in place with the wrinkles of her grin. Her chin had stopped its constant chewing movement. Her hands that drew these old beads through them as she taught me about the mysteries of the rosary were now so clean and white I could almost see through them. When I ran to the bed to hug and kiss her she had turned into stone, cold, hard, not answering. All of her, even her hands that had so often rubbed my face when answering my questions about my father. The only thing left was the creak in the bed.

A fresh cry just like that of a new kid goat came through the kitchen from the new room. The shouting had stopped. Brad eased himself around the door and gently closed it behind him. We looked at each other: tears in his eyes softening his craggy face.

'Is she all right, Brad! Is Mammy all right?'

He came towards me and gathered me to him. 'You did a great job, young Cormac. Yes; she's grand, and she has just brought you . . . ' He was surprised when I pulled away from hearing about this sister but he grabbed my hands. 'You have a brother, young Cormac, a fine strong lad the image of yourself.'

The good news hopping off the bad stunned me like a dazzled rabbit. I climbed into my sleepy bed in the loft.

Stepper running at the gate, rising. Now I know what it feels like for Santa soaring in that sleigh: Nurse Relihan, my bag of toys; Granny Rua, a soaring eagle.

I am on her back, soaring, circling over Highgrove Manor, over the Glens, the Owmore river an ocean in the divide between. I awoke to the snuggly feeling of a gentle hand rubbing my forehead. The smiling angel's face of cousin Breda Brosnan, Mammy's bridesmaid, framed by her soft sandy curls, leaned down and kissed me.

'So how's my tired cousin Cormac this morning?'

'Not tired now; you heard about Granny Rua?'

'Yes; she was my Aunt Niamh. Did you know that?'

'Where's everyone? The house is too quiet.'

'Now you're awake, come on down to your breakfast and we'll have a chat.'

I knew by the look on her that it was nothing bad because there was no botheration spoiling the light in her eyes. I pulled on my pants, took my shirt and skated down the ladder after her; then straight out the door to wash myself from the barrel in the yard. She thought what I was doing was very funny but then it was easy to amuse Breda. Mammy had told me she was training to be a teacher in Limerick and would be coming to a school near home after the summer holidays.

I checked the old room. Granny Rua was gone. I was running to the new room when Breda caught me and explained that everyone had gone to the chapel for a Mass for Granny Rua before laying her to rest in the cemetery.

'What about Mammy and my brother?'

'Your little brother is asleep in the crib. I've just changed him and settled him. Your Mammy and Brad won't be long. We can see them at the cemetery from the top field soon if you stop talking and have your breakfast.'

She had mixed my porridge with cream and honey so I was soon shining the bowl to capture all the taste. 'You seem to like it, young Cormac?'

'It's nice in the mouth, but that's the way with everything you make.'

'Well, thank you,' she laughed.

Two heifers I hadn't seen before were looking for something they couldn't find in our back field.

'Was it you brought them, Breda?'

'Some people came last night while you were asleep; 'twas they brought them.'

'Why?'

We sized each other up for a moment. I waited.

'Aunty Niamh would have been very happy at what happened last night. Those men were sent from Highgrove Manor to lift her over the pain of the deaths of her husband and Ellen and your father, the wild one.'

'Why are you saying that about my father? I thought you were a nice lady!'

'Sorry, Cormac. He was not wild in a bad way. What got him into trouble was his way of making everyone else's troubles his own. The burden of tradition, I suppose; it's expected of the MacRuas.'

'Why?'

'You're only a boy; soon enough you'll know.'

She made herself busy though there didn't seem to be any need for it.

I had to find out what my dad was really like. 'So he was very brave, wasn't he, my dad?'

'A pity he didn't know himself a bit better. My mother says there will never be another like him.'

I could see she thought I wasn't ready to give any more information so we took my little brother up to the field.

The village of Benmore kept itself to the Hare Mountain side of Owmore river, around a church with the cemetery stretched out behind. Breda allowed me to hold my brother for the first time as we stood there and watched the crowd almost filling the cemetery.

'She's happy now, my Aunty Niamh; she's with her beloved Brad again and Ellen and Cormac. Even the gentry came to send her off.'

So what will Brad do now, I wondered. Things he pictured in his head might now happen in reality without his mother to question him. But I couldn't talk to Breda about things like that. Instead I took the opportunity to pose my question as I handed back my brother.

'No one has taken Mammy's place in Heather Hill; did Uncle Peter ask you to marry him yet?'

'Did he say he was going to?'

'He promised he was going to, and he had better not pick this to be his first promise to break.'

In accordance with tradition my brother was christened Laurence, after Granpa Healy, our mother's father. He really was a joker from the time he could move around on his own. His shortened name of Laurie fitted him well. Anything he could pick up in his hands he tried for taste in his mouth, even the tiny round goat's droppings to be found every morning around the yard. On his second birthday I took him for a bareback ride on Stepper. Loopy had grown very fond of him even though Laurie pulled his hair, so she jumped on to the pony's back just behind us. Stepper laid back her ears and didn't seem to like it at first but she quickly adapted to the routine. When I told Mammy and Brad they had to see it to believe it, and then Brad and I worked out a plan to take the trick further.

Brad had a system of whistle commands which would send Loopy off up the Glens to collect the sheep, goats or cows. He could also send him home from the Glens and get him to stay. So Laurie and I rode off to the top field with Loopy riding behind as usual. There we got off and Brad whistled his come-home signal.

Loopy jumped back on Stepper's back; we climbed a stile and waited. Brad called again. Loopy jumped off and walked away, obviously waiting for Stepper and ourselves to follow. About halfway down the field Loopy turned around and gave a few anxious whines. Stepper look around at us, walked off a few paces, looked again and then set off at a gallop after Loopy. A few minutes later, at Brad's signal, they were back to collect us.

Brad decided it was time to select a new pup from the many offers of dogs that came his way. He explained that because Loopy was in his prime and proving to have excellent reactions, inclination to learn and loyalty to commands, we should get a well-bred bitch to breed off him.

The spark was back in life after Granny Rua. Yet something was missing in all I was learning, something I yearned to know, to make a part of me. I couldn't find words to ask what it was and where or whom should I ask. At school it seemed that it should be at home. The breeze of activity at home was too great for me to ask a question that wasn't ripe.

THREE

Summers were full of things happening. While we were on holidays at Healys', Uncle Danny's forge became the centre of the world. Near the forge Uncle Peter and Granpa made a new house rise out of the ruins of the adjacent old stone terrace where the people had been burned out by the Black and Tans soon after Peter and Danny were born.

When I was eleven Danny showed me how to make myself useful in the forge and promised to take me dazzling rabbits with him at night if I mastered the skill of removing the worn shoes from the quiet horses, and afterwards cleaning their hooves. I turned the handle on the bellows and watched the red iron from the fire being formed into horseshoes on the anvil. Danny would always temper and finish the shoes as the iron obeyed his powerful hammer.

I gradually came to understand the fitting process as he rested the hot shoe against the hoof and trimmed or carved the necessary adjustments to make the perfect fit. The swirling sniffiness of different smokes made a tingle in the world of the forge.

Using Brad's methods, I found that I could gradually get the wild or timid horses to stand still and look back into my eyes. Then I'd coax them to follow the nodding of my head with theirs. I was hoping Danny wouldn't notice. A thrill tingled inside my skin when I patted the curious face and neck and on down the foreleg to the hoof. Danny showed me how to take the hoof into my leather apron in the straddle between my legs.

Old Leftie Casey was a blacksmith who had come with Danny from the Farrs of Blackwater (Granma Healy's people). That summer Leftie too spent most of his time trimming stones with his hammer where Danny's house would stand. Now and again his tall figure would shuffle into the forge usually to light his pipe and he would remark with a throaty laugh, 'Heh, heh, heh; 'tis a wonder they wouldn't take off their own shoes for you, ladeen.'

I exulted in the wonders for my eyes, the smells for my nostrils, the mixture of sounds, the feel of the horses; so much life in so small a space. And afterwards the aroma and taste of Granma Healy's cooking to soothe the hunger of the day.

In the forge Laurie stopped being a baby after he learned that his fingers were softer than a hammer and that some black bits of iron were sizzling surprises. We both had to wear boots there. Granma Healy had bought a pair for each of us before she left on a pilgrimage to Knock. The worst thing about the forge was having to get into the zinc bath for a scrubbing from Mammy every night after she brought us home. At times like that I had pity for Laurie having to get into that bath with me but I was glad he was there to take Mammy's attention away from me. The soap would pierce his tired eyes; often he was already asleep in the trap on the way home to Heather Hill with Mammy and Granpa.

Wet days were always busy in the forge and the day that Brad arrived with the bogoak heads for Danny's windows and doors didn't seem to be much good for anything except shoeing horses and building houses. I liked the look in Brad's eyes when he gathered Laurie and me to him before jumping the fence to meet the men who were waiting for the bogoak from the Glens. A good job he had made friends with Mammy after I had heard them arguing about each other's families, I thought; otherwise they would have had a long wait for Brad to arrive.

The air around him was dancing to music I couldn't hear. Laurie held my hand and said, 'Daddy' as we watched two elderly men wipe tears from their eyes with their caps as they shook a hand each. Some straightened their backs and announced to each other that no Kerryman would ever be more welcome than Brad MacRua in County Cork's village of Knockeen. It was as if they owed him something and knew that he would not accept payment.

Stepper had half the soot licked off Laurie's face to check that it really was him by the time Granpa came to collect us in his trap. Granma Healy was to be met at the station on her way home from her pilgrimage, and there were things to do. Our joy in seeing Breda Brosnan waiting in the yard soon flattened when she started filling the zinc bath to wash us. Laurie didn't seem too fussy but while I was very fond of Breda it didn't extend to having her pawing all over my naked body, especially down low where the hot water made something rise that I didn't want her to see. She got a great laugh with Mammy out of what they called my modesty, so I was left to get along with my own scrubbing.

True to form, after he was dried and fed, Laurie fell asleep and Mammy settled him in bed in the loft. I set off with Granpa to meet Granma Healy. The engine whistled louder and longer than usual as the train approached the station.

'You'd think 'twas the Kerry team going through after winning the All-Ireland,' he remarked.

But when the train emptied its excitement on to the platform, 'It's a miracle – Mary Healy's tongue is loosened,' the chant rose out of the babble as Granma was ushered towards us. The poor woman didn't have a word in her. She gathered me to her and pecked a quick kiss on to Granpa's lips as the train whistled its way towards Killarney.

'What are they talking about, *a chroi*?' Granpa wondered, giving her his red handkerchief to dry her eyes when we were clear of the excitement.

Sure enough her tongue was loosened. It laboured around her mouth to form the words 'Lo-oey' and 'u Co-mac' as she pointed at Granpa and me respectively.

He drew the pony to a stop. 'Well praise be to God. I never thought I'd see the day you'd say my name or anyone else's name, not that it mattered. Well praise be to God, my Mary.'

They hugged each other for a long time, almost as if they were young like Mammy and Brad.

'What do you think of that, young Cormac? You'll be out of a job now, little man. Well praise be to God! Wait until Deirdre and the two boyos hear this! Well praise be to God! Hey-up there, pony; won't we have a happy house tonight?'

I knew by the feel of the next morning that the cock's crowing had failed to make an impression on my slumber. Two strange sounds teased my ears from the kitchen. Laurie became aware of the day as I got out of the bed; so he joined me in exploring the new noises. The first one was easy; Grandma's loosened tongue was slapping around in her mouth trying to produce sounds familiar to her ear. But her mouth stumbled as it struggled to dance in time with her ear.

Laurie slid down the spiral banister to get hold of what appeared to be a young silver fox snuggled in Grandma's lap nodding his head to the stroking of her fingers. While Laurie and the fox sized each other up I learned that it was a shepherd pup whose grandmother was a fox tamed by Jockey Jack, a little dancer from the hill. Brad would take her home and get her used to Loopy so that I could join him in giving her a name and training her to work to signals I would learn to give.

'So she'll be my dog if she'll be working to my whistle?' Brad nodded. The thrill of having a living thing to call my own was new and nice. Laurie liked it too.

'All right, Laurie, we'll share the pup and we'll have to think of a nice name for her.'

'Why can't we call her Puppy?' Laurie wondered.

'Why don't we call her Polka after her owner's favourite dance?' I asked. Brad nodded.

Mammy and Peter were in the kitchen when I was taking Laurie to bed that night. Their conversation, started by Mammy, shocked me into realising how mistaken I was about Breda and Peter.

'Will that house be finished by Shrove, do you think?'

'Ah, 'twill be roofed in a few weeks, after that we'll have the wind at our backs.'

'Because if it isn't finished by Shrove, Breda won't be marching to the altar rails.'

'Well I suppose that's understandable enough but she shouldn't fret. 'Twill be finished for Christmas.'

Now there was a very strange face on things. The house was Uncle Danny's and there was no word about him getting married. Now Breda wouldn't walk up the aisle until the house was finished on time, so it must be Danny she was about to marry. That still left the problem of replacing Mammy at Heather Hill and Peter was showing no urgency at all about the matter. And the idea of Breda and Danny seemed to fit as well as a left foot in a right shoe. Contrary to what Breda thought I obviously hadn't done enough, so I would have to square Peter's impressions with Breda's to put a more fitting face on affairs. Mammy would just have to be replaced at Heather Hill by Breda, the only one who could come near such a role.

The long summer stretch had knocked the fun out of my stay at Heather Hill. It was our second home, no longer our first: great for a visit of a week or two, and the forge was magic, but it was not home.

These holidays would end in twelve days, twelve days to get Uncle Peter to marry Breda and put matters right. Twelve days to agree about a name for our new pup that Brad would teach me to train. Twelve days to get the tip of Granma Healy's tongue to touch the right part of her mouth to produce the words she wanted.

Opportunity presented itself when Breda visited Knockeen to inspect progress on Danny's house the day she was returning to Killarney. Peter was topping off a chimney, Leftie was finishing the last horse, so Danny came back into the forge. He owed me a favour.

'Remember at the start of the holidays you promised that you'd teach me how to dazzle and snare rabbits if I learned to prepare the quiet horses' hooves?'

'Yes, I did. I promised that. And now that you can shoe an odd horse as well I'd better take you out and show you, although the nights are very short for dazzling – you'd need the long dark nights for that.'

'Snaring then; that'll do for a start.'

'Right, snaring it is; that'll do until your next holidays at Hallowe'en. We'll have dark nights then for dazzling, and hungry rabbits looking for leafy nibbles.'

'I didn't know you were thinking of getting married, Uncle Danny?'

'Begod neither did I, young Cormac; what gave you that impression?'

'There seems to be an awful hurry to get your house finished by Shrove.' He lifted his cap and eyebrows. 'It's only your house the rush is about. Breda can't get married to herself, or to the priest . . . '

'Ah, that's where you'd want to be careful now.' He laughed; 'You see; marriage is a very serious thing for a woman; she's not only marrying her man but setting up home as well. 'Tis bad enough setting up house with the old people still in it, but very few women would be up to nesting while brothers or sisters of her husband were still in the coop.' He looked at me while I teased out the meaning of his riddle in my mind.

'Oh, so 'tis Peter she'll be marrying after all, so?'

'Well, it won't be me. I'm grand the way I am, not ready for a big step like that yet. Hey, where are you going? Be careful, they might be talking – or something.'

Outside I saw that the chimney seemed to be as finished as the one at the other end of the house but Granpa was up there scratching and shaping with his trowel. On the ground Peter's pipe was nowhere to be seen as he leaned against a wall listening to Breda.

'You're very fond of Breda, aren't you, Uncle Peter?'

'Ah, you're a terrible man, young Cormac, a holy terror altogether.'

'And you're very fond of Uncle Peter, aren't you, Breda?'

A warm Granny-Rua look came over her and she gathered me to her, teasing my hair. 'I think it's only fair after all your trouble, young Cormac, that you should be the first to know. The first Saturday next February is the day we'll be married.'

I caught a glimpse of Uncle Peter's face; he was very much in agreement with that.

Granma Healy borrowed my mouth and signed words and phrases for me to speak. It was as if she had baby equipment in an old mouth. Sometimes we would repeat a word over and over again. Then she would hug me when she got it right.

Danny enjoyed my wanting to recognise the difference between a live and a dead track, and at what point of the track to set the snare. In the evening we would set ten snares each and compare catches on our return every morning; Danny was as unhappy with his nine as I was delighted with my first five, which gradually improved.

FOUR

Easter Monday, 1952: the Republic of Ireland is three years old after centuries of labour to win back its own identity. Even younger than Laurie, I thought. Something itches Brad inside his cloak of pride. The ground has been prepared for the setting of the oats but he says that can wait for an ordinary day like tomorrow. The significance of today has to be contemplated.

He measures out his steps as we make our way to the forest. It is much different by day. Across on Hare Mountain spring is budding around Highgrove Manor. He selects a sally rod and cuts it from its trunk with his knife. Eyes fixed on the manor, he begins paring the rod, looking, paring, not looking at the rod, narrowing his eyes on his target. Shavings spill from the rod. 'Up the Republic' hisses through his teeth.

'You want to know what really happened?' he asked as he selected another rod.

'But you told me, about old Brad and the pistol . . . '

'You know what murder is? Learned that in school, didn't you?'

'Old Brad murdered?'

'By Squire's father or his lackeys; planted a locked pistol in his hand, and shot him.'

The shavings were now thinner, slower, more deliberate. My mouth hung open, so I must have asked why.

'Your Aunt Ellen; Squire's father raped her.'

I thought about cousin Breda; so like Aunt Ellen, people said.

Attacked in whatever vicious way it meant to be raped. He was speaking again.

'So when my father faced old Squire about it, they had to kill him or be killed.'

'But Aunt Ellen; they can't just kill people like that?'

'Ah, they have power over the Law. They put out a rumour that she'd killed herself. Depressed, they said, after the shock of her father.' He bent the rod; it snapped. 'Knowledge, that's what killed her. She told us, your father and me, told us what they had done. They didn't want her talking.'

Later we looked across at where it happened, the cliff a mass of rhododendron shimmering in the sun. 'So my father tried to do something about it and they killed him too?'

'That leaves it up to us, doesn't it; the new republic.'

He moved among the trees, felled a thistle with a single kick, ordered the dogs to stay and released a leveret from a tangle of briars.

'But we're not going to kill anyone?' I couldn't hold the question in any longer.

He spoke about the edge and sparkle there was to life with my father, how their views had differed.

Dad had wanted to tackle the squire at an intellectual level, even debated relevant issues with him to soften him up for the big one. Later Brad said: 'No; we won't kill the bastard. Just find a way we can make his life hell.'

What Brad was suggesting seemed to be right. Revenge. Wash the blood of our family clean. But it did not fit in with the message of Christ which I was learning at school as the master prepared us for confirmation. And Christ died for his message, for everyone including the squire. I wondered if my father had thought about that.

'Time to get the anvil out of your ears and become a bit more of what's native to you,' was how Brad introduced me to his greater demands of another winter. He outlined what the prize in the spring would be. I would get to feel the salmon under water and learn to distinguish the cock from the hen. I wouldn't be allowed to attempt a catch until after my fourteenth birthday. By then I should have built the strength to go with my knowledge and skill.

The first week was hard on our dogs Loopy and Polka. They had to learn the signals to execute new night commands. It must have been harder on them not to chase a hare or a rabbit while carrying out their commands than it would be for a boy to disregard a bouncing ball. But at Brad's command Loopy would find me in the forest just as Polka would locate Brad among the reeds by the Glen streams, regardless of how dark or defiant the night.

On one such night I was writing an essay in Irish on the subject of 'My Father' as part of my home exercise. My real though dead father was the one I had chosen to write about, not Brad, the man in his place. This was not just any essay. I felt as if he was looking over my shoulder. He filled his place in our family. It was like that feeling in the forge with the horses for the first time. He gushed through my pencil.

I was well into the third page when Brad opened the kitchen door to allow a squally gale in before him. He held it shut. 'Come on, you can do that any time; 'tis time to go.'

'But I have to hand it up to the master tomorrow, and I'm nearly finished.'

'This is more important; get your skins on; we have to go, now.' He was dragging me away from my father.

'No, this is important now. I'll be ready soon.'

The change in the clicks of Mammy's knitting needles betrayed her unease in the corner. I returned to my dad.

'That's right,' Brad rejoined; 'put the book learning above its rightful place; dream ideas beyond yourself, just like your father.'

'Can't you get ready yourself, Brad,' she pleaded. 'He'll need his book learning to make sense of what we can't teach him for the kind of a world he's growing into. He'll be ready soon: I'll see to it.'

"Tis wrong for a woman to get into men's affairs she knows nothing about.' The door opened and quickly closed behind him.

'I'm sorry, Mammy; I didn't mean to turn him on you.'

'I'll call you early in the morning to finish that. What's it about anyway?'

'It's about my father.'

'Oh, Mother of God! Don't tell him that's what was holding you. Get your skins on and go after him. I'll call you early to finish it. And I wish I knew what was so important about going out on a night that was howling at everyone to stay inside.'

As my eyes adjusted to the darkness I could see the antlers swinging behind his shoulders. He was wearing the red-deer skin – going for a catch. It would be a night in the mouth of danger. I could hear the special sheepskin footwear with the bone grips on the soles.

Though he crept along by the hedges I had to work at keeping up with him. What seemed to be a cold night at first was warming up inside my goatskins, inside my heavy cap Mammy had knitted and the new rubber boots Uncle Danny bought me. The dogs had been ordered to stay home. We scaled the cliff on to the plateau between the two waterfalls, a great sweep where the forest petered out to clumps of ferns, heather and furze bushes.

I knew every detail of these wild heights in daylight. The mountain gorge followed two hollows after tumbling over the first waterfall and came together again to power wash the rocks going down the second, beside where the road surrendered to a track in its struggle to climb over the mountain from the Glens.

Brad drew me to a squatting position beside him in the ferns to make sure I understood his instructions. He would follow the gorge to the pool in the hollow. I would take up my hiding place in the furze bushes out of the direct line of the waterfalls, from where in daylight I could see the end of the road. Even though it was a little out of season we would use the bullfinch style to whistle our signals.

Because of the darkness and the gusting wind I would have to be alert to every sound that did not belong to the night. Any one of them could herald a bailiff trying to outguess Brad MacRua and become the first to catch a Brad of any generation in action.

I settled in the bushes and got the relative locations of my surroundings in place in my mind's eye just as I had done when Brad had trained me with the blindfold last March. Then we had been further down the Glens with only the rain to distort the night sounds.

I figured that the bailiff couldn't come up the way we came, so his likely approach would either be from the end of the road below me or by one of the tracks through the mountain pass coming on to the upper waterfall.

The wind was gusting from the southwest, making it impossible to pick up stealthy sounds from up there but much easier to hear anything happening on the road. I had to pick out an horizon with my eyes now adjusted to the darkness. I scanned for signs of any movement. Soon I noticed the absence of local sounds. The few living sounds came from where the forest ended further down the Glens. A stirring on the upper horizon concentrated my wits. It was probably a goat or maybe a deer, soon joined by others on the rim. They must have picked up something on the wind, I figured. And then I picked it up, the movement of a dog accompanied by the whiff of liniment and carbolic soap.

'Man and dog,' I whistled in the direction of the pool. I strained to pick up a response.

'Send dog on chase,' the bullfinch replied on the double.

About a furlong away a stone scurried from an unintended kick while the sheep and goats gathered round my bush on the arrival of Rex, the bailiff's German shepherd I had got to know so well. He had even picked up the gist of two whistle signals: 'Go fetch!' and 'Go on guard!'

The curious animals on the horizon were joined by the commanding outline of a stag. Rex came to me well ahead of his owner, stealing along a track rounding towards our plateau. I pointed him towards the upper horizon and waited for his ears to signal that he had picked out the stag and companions.

'Go fetch!'

'Dog or me?' from the bullfinch.

'Dog.'

'Go fetch!' I pointed towards the horizon. I mingled with the sheep and goats around me. 'Go fetch!'

He dashed off, hesitated, returned. Brad would be aware of his movement. The bailiff panted on to the plateau downwind, calling 'Rex' in between gasps. Again I pointed: 'Go fetch! Go fetch!' I hoped his owner wouldn't check out my cover of sheep and goats. Rex understood.

'Man here,' I whistled.

The bullfinch fell silent. Bailiff crouched and stole towards the pool.

'Man rounding,' I whistled into the wind. On the horizon only the stag was left.

'Man there, me here. Come down in hide.' The bullfinch whistled from upwind towards the edge of the forest.

The bailiff was intent on his quarry near the pool. The stag moved around but remained faithful to the horizon. I eased my way over the edge and down between the rocks on the steep face towards the ferns. From there I knew the track that would lead me into the forest.

'Me here,' I whistled towards the forest.

'Home yourself in hide; no call if no danger.'

The bullfinch was prancing ahead.

In the forest the howls of the wind were reduced to whispers and creaks. New feelings crept in under the tingle of the earlier excitement. I longed for some living creature to join in the sense of achievement bubbling through me. In my mind's eye I saw Laurie sprawled in the bed and Polka awaiting our return home.

The wolf. Surely they see him, the man and the girl. The wolf, the teeth, the knife-blade jutting from his stomach. Tongue, teeth; red, white. Girl, Breda, why are you not afraid? Fair wavy hair. Singing. Floating on the cadence. Plucked; wolf's paw a hairy hand, tickling her, laughing. Teeth biting the laugh in her mouth. Snipping scissors cutting her stomach. Screaming. Teeth frightening her scream to silence. Cutting, cutting. Blood. A tiny wolf inside her stomach. Scissors gone. Whimpering; crying. Daddy; Daddy. The man holding her, covering her blood. Tiny wolf eating, growing bigger, from the girl's stomach into the man. Gnawing, eating the man's heart.

'Cormac! Cormac! It's all right, Cormac.' I grab her, cling to Mammy, dry my sweat on her cotton nightdress.

She draws my head into the gap between her breasts, and kisses my damp hair. A mug of camomile tea and the safe care oozing through her hands banish my terror.

After what seemed like minutes she coaxed me into the morning. It was essay time. Later at breakfast Brad made no reference to the night before but spoke of going to Heather Hill or Knockeen to do an exchange with Danny.

'See if you can exchange for some vegetables too, so I can make more things happen in the stew,' Mammy said. The sows had broken into the garden, followed by the goats. Between them they had cleaned out most of her vegetables and herbs.

Out in a special rolled section in the hay, before I left for school, he showed me two fourteen-pound cocks, the catch from the previous night. I marvelled at how he had moved with the extra weight. He wanted to know if there was any event of the night that frightened me or left me unsure of what to do. I assured him that once I adjusted to the conditions there was no real bother, and wondered why he hadn't told Mammy what had happened.

'Maybe this is a good time for you to learn this – and I mean learn it not to forget: never tell a woman what you don't want others to know.'

'But she's Mammy . . .' I thought of old Brad at the lake with Granny Rua when they were young.

'She's a woman. Rules have served our family for generations. Rules keep the bailiff from getting too close to us.'

'That bailiff last night got close.'

'You'll see closer than that, and when the time comes you'll know what to do. Remember: keep your mouth shut.'

'Children too?' He nodded.

'No brave stories for Laurie or at school neither.'

School was asking questions of another side of my world. I was now over halfway through my time with the master and had adjusted to his subtle easygoing ways, contrasting with the almost constant talking, explaining, questioning, shouting and threatening of the teachers in the other two classrooms.

The master was tall and lean with tawny-grey hair curling over his ears and collar and smoked a straight-stemmed pipe. During singing classes his long bony fingers had his fiddle singing along with us. The previous year he had offered lessons on how to play to anyone with the *grá* or desire to learn. Something about him tempted me to try his offer, just to get to know him better, especially after his reaction to my essay about my father. He seemed to have known Dad very well, and I felt he could fill in the gaps in Brad's hints as to what was expected of me. Each class got an essay in Irish and English to complete every week, to be handed up for correction two days after it was given. There were four classes in his room, fourth, fifth, sixth, and seventh for those pupils who wanted to prepare for county-council or other scholarships into secondary school. From Monday to Thursday he dealt with an Irish essay for one class and an English essay for another. His way of doing this encouraged us to do our best.

The twelve of us in sixth class would gather around his table where he would give back our essays showing corrections in grammar, spelling and punctuation, together with marks out of ten in red pencil.

As I was last to enrol in the class my essay would be dealt with just after Betsy Foran, with whom I still shared a seat. She painted a detailed picture of what her father wore, the colour of his hair and eyes and I learned that he was the only boy in a family of thirteen. But her final sentence defined the importance of Brad's stress on secrecy.

'My Daddy is a water bailiff and he loves his work because he saves the fish in the river from poachers and bad people fishing without the squire's permission.'

Like most of the other essays hers got six out of ten.

During that last sentence the Master removed his jacket and puckered his lips. A smile rested in the eyes watching my face from under his raised eyebrows.

'Ah, sure, good girl, Betsy. There are bailiffs and poachers and hounds and foxes, and thanks be to God for the very clever foxes that help the balance of nature.'

The six on my essay was turned upside down, and even though I had more pages and a different treatment to the others, my father obviously was a lot different and much more exciting than theirs. The highest I had heard up to now was an eight from a girl in seventh on why she wanted to be a teacher. The master had sat her on the table to read her essay to the classroom.

'All right so; you can all go back to your places now.' His long fingers curled around my arm as he continued. 'Now young Cormac MacRua of the Glens is going to read his essay about a man who died before he was born: his own father.'

I found myself sitting on the table looking out at forty-seven expressions varying from curiosity to sneering.

The master paused in the act of lighting his pipe from a taper out of the fire. 'When you're settled, young Cormac, you can begin.'

With that encouragement I began: 'The man who was my father never knew me, but I am getting to know him. In a way I have two fathers. There's Brad, my father's twin brother, and my real father who was killed before my mother married Brad MacRua here in the Glens.

'I can see what my father would have looked like because very few could make out the difference between himself and Brad. But there were differences between them as people, in the way they saw things and in how they reacted to them. It was through my mother I first began to know my father. When I would ask a question about him she would change, and get hold of me and straighten my clothes or lick her hand to clean my face. I like what that change does to her. She has told me many stories about

56

him; the one with the most meaning has no words but tells me that for my mother there will never be anyone like my father.

'Little bits of him come to me at different times from Brad. It started with what my father would do, usually at times when things needed to be done. Later he told me why and how he died or was murdered. People say that Highgrove Manor will have no luck for that.

'There was a long night before my mother and Brad got married when my two grannies spoke through me about my father and his father as men in the eyes of their own women. Up until that night I carried a bitterness against the people who killed my father.

'I even blamed him for placing himself in such danger without seeming to know he was there. But I know now that's not the way it was. I learned it from those two women at either side of that hearth. They didn't realise they were telling me because they have never been caught in the thrill of squatting within feet of danger and his dog.

'I know that my father's time in this world made a difference to many people. They believed in him at a safe distance. He added to the good name of our family, a name greater than Highgrove Manor since the famine of a hundred years ago when Great-grandfather Brad MacRua showed a parish how to help nature to provide for its people.'

I looked across at the master but his thoughts seemed to have drifted off on the smoke from his pipe. I eased myself off the table to scowls from some of the boys and smiles from Mags-the-well and Margaret Wally. Betsy Foran gave an impression of a rattlesnake with her tongue. I must have overdone my reaction with a searching glare on to which I forced a smile. Now she used her tongue to more lethal effect. 'Your father! If he was such a great man why didn't he marry your mother?'

The meek Betsy had turned into a shrew and hurt in ways new to me. Billy-the-bully and Christy Leahy turned around to drive her message home.

'So now, boys and girls, there's a lad that knows his father better than most of you, though he never met him. Not worth a cap of crabs some of your fathers aren't, pampered and spoilt by your mothers. Spoilt just like they were by their own mothers. 'Tis unknown how many talented women are wasted on useless men.'

He stopped to take a mug of water out of the bucket.

Some of the eyes trained on me betrayed the hatred of a terrier for a rat. I hoped he would go away from my essay on to anything else.

After what seemed ages the master continued: 'So now, boys and girls, your next essay will be on the subject of *Mo Mháthair – My Mother;* that'll give most of you better material to work with.'

Over the next four weeks I had to keep what was happening to me in the schoolyard from Mammy and Brad. Despite the mild autumn travelling into December to see what Christmas was like, I had taken to wearing my boots and kept my shins covered with my socks as a protection against the kicking and stomping to which I was being treated, and to hide the effects. Billy-the-bully's popularity had soared for the number of times he kicked the legs from under me and then fell on me along with the bulky Christy Leahy.

To be sat on the table to read your essay was showing up too many people; to be sat there twice was asking for trouble. But my mother was worth every bit of it.

The boys had the use of the small field sloping away from the back of the school while the girls and younger boys played in the side and front yards.

The master always went home for his lunch, so the three bullies and their followers could mete out their punishment without fear of interference.

The threat of similar treatment awaited those who might defend me. Shades of black, blue, red and dirty yellow exchanged places on my limbs and body, so that I had to be careful not to strip in the sight of Laurie or anybody. Sleep stayed away at night while I tried possible courses of action. Telling anybody was out; fighting back was just what they wanted. In the darkness I allowed my mind to float over scenarios in which I raced the bullies up the Glens at night, right into the quagmires on the way. I would drift off to sleep on the balm of their pleas for help only to awaken to the pain of my bruises and the frustration of my inaction facing into another day. Then I thought of a plan.

'I was wondering when this was going to happen. So now, could Betsy and Christy and, of course, Billy honour us with their presence around the blackboard.' The Master waited.

Betsy had been copying the answers to my sums for weeks and then passed on the answers to Christy and Billy. I had decided to write the questions of the previous evening on to my page in reverse order. Betsy hadn't noticed this when copying the answers. She gaped at me, while Billy and Christy scowled.

The master turned the blackboard around to show the sums he had given us to work on.

He offered the chalk to each of them in turn. Betsy attempted to say something but he stopped her.

'So now, here are your sheets of paper with the answers you wrote down?'

'Yes, Sir,' from the three who were not enjoying their situation.

'So now, let's have a look at our six sums again, and the answers from our geniuses.'

$$14 \times \qquad 17 \times \qquad 22 \times \qquad 19 \times \qquad 13 \times \qquad 15 \times$$
$$\underline{13} \qquad \underline{11} \qquad \underline{16} \qquad \underline{18} \qquad \underline{14} \qquad \underline{21}$$
$$315 \qquad 182 \qquad 342 \qquad 352 \qquad 187 \qquad 182$$

A hint of a giggle started in seventh class like a flame in a piece of bracken, then crackled through sixth class and roared into life through fifth into fourth, warming the faces at the blackboard to a glowing redness. Betsy bawled. She rushed back to her seat and buried her face in her hands. The master took a seasoned sally rod from the top of the press and placed it on the table before writing the correct answers under the incorrect ones, and pointing out the reverse pattern. Again he picked up the sally rod and quieted the giggles with a rare chilly look through the room.

The colour left Billy's face. A wet patch formed in front of his trousers and the wet trickled into his boots. Christy requested, and was granted, permission to go out to the toilet but he seemed to have left it too late.

The master returned the rod to the top of the press and sent Billy back to his place. 'So now: Betsy copied from Cormac and then our two big boyos copied from Betsy. Would I be right?'

'Yes, sir?' from Billy. Betsy nodded through her sobs.

Christy walked back in with a sickly expression on his face, his legs well apart.

'So now, my brave Billy and my bold Christy, you can't spend the day here in that state. Off home now both of you, and don't forget to tell your mothers and fathers. And remember, a pig should never try to outwit a fox.'

They took his advice but other bullies took their place.

The nights with Brad built on each other towards my fourteenth birthday. He had taken five salmon from the streams of the Glens and brought me deeper into his world of nature and the fish.

Tensions between us had been smoothed by his understanding of my school problems.

Laurie was brought into the rim of our world in the forest. Loopy and Polka joined in the daylight fun of gathering cones, leaves, twigs and bracken for the fires in the house but most would go into the special tunnel where the hill joined the gable of the piggery. Only Brad and I knew about this (and maybe Mammy). Here on humid misty days we would position our layers for smoking.

After we got them smouldering we would top them off with layers of mouldy hay and straw. Over that we would already have suspended our salmon, strips of bacon, venison and occasional items such as eels and ribs.

We would then crawl back out and fill up the gap with stones. In the mist and fog only the keenest eye could detect the controlled escape of grey smoke.

The smell from the piggery countered any giveaway aromas.

I became involved in Brad's method of distribution of his surplus. A culled stag or doe would nourish the table for several families. We would divide it out for a house in each of the surrounding four townlands. Some would always go to Heather Hill, especially any surplus of the smoked goods, which Mammy carefully wrapped in bleached flour-sacking. It was while I was being dispatched with such a bundle after school on a Friday evening in the middle of January 1953 that she urged me to return as early as possible the next day, just in case. She was expecting another baby, so I took it that I might have to journey again in the trap to collect Nurse Relihan. Darkness was a friend on my journey to Heather Hill. I sometimes walked, sometimes ran with my feelings, my thoughts. The fuss Granma Healy made, now that she could speak, melted away another bad week at school. The lovely state of the house reminded me that it was ready with Uncle Peter to welcome Cousin Breda as the new woman-of-the-house in a few weeks.

After I was settled in bed in the loft Granma Healy came to tell me she would rouse me early in the morning for Granpa to drive me home in the trap.

'Can you remember when you were at school, Granma?'

'Sure I'm still learning, young Cormac; why so?'

'Did people, any of the older children, pick on you because you couldn't speak, or for no reason?'

She eased herself on to the edge of the bed. I could see Mammy's comforting look on her face in the candlelight.

'Ah but I didn't go to ordinary school at the start. I went to a school for children like myself. We learned together from the nuns. We learned everything; they were so kind with their time. Then we would help to teach the younger ones. Our sign teacher was English, so we never learned Irish. Anyhow, that was how it was. It would be a lot different for you, of course?'

'Yes, well it is. The school itself is fine; the master is grand and he's even better at teaching the fiddle. But sometimes a couple of older boys pick on me. I'm not the only one, of course. If the master gives out to them they pick on someone. And of course Brad warned me, well 'twas about being caught in another type of tight corner, never to hit back directly. So they know I won't fight and they take no notice of the names I call them. So they jeer and boast that the great Cormac MacRua's son is nothing but a yellow coward.'

'And has Brad said anything about anything else?'

I couldn't fit a lie into eyes like hers.

'Well; the murders . . . '

'Oh my God,' she said.

She took out her beads and began saying the rosary as she

patted my hair and face with her left hand.

It felt like it was around the end of the first decade that she called me to get ready for the road home. The flour on her hands and apron and the aroma from the kitchen down below told me her morning had an early start on the day.

It was the first time since her pilgrimage that she would be away from home for a few days. Much to Peter's annoyance she plied him with directions as to how to sustain himself and Granpa in her absence. Then it was off to Knockeen village to leave fresh bread and smoked tasties from the sack to Danny in his new house, in case he was visited by starvation in her absence. There was a roughness about the new house, as there was about Danny himself – a lack of a woman's touch, Granma said. She promised again that after Peter's wedding she would spend more time on trying to make a home out of Danny's house.

Danny agreed with Granpa that there was a hard spell of black frost on the way, so the pony was to be reshod. As I pared down her hooves I imagined I was working on the feet of Tinker Burke and Bolg Sweeney from sixth, the two who made trouble for anyone younger or smarter. Tinker got his name from the time he wandered off with a camp of travellers who plied their trade making and repairing tin ponnies and saucepans nearby for a few weeks before travelling on towards the next horizon.

His widowed father's relief waned when Tinker arrived home a week later, rejected by the camp because he caused too much trouble, ate too much and wouldn't work. His mousy hair was shorn close to a dirty scabby scalp. At close quarters both he and the even bigger Bolg Sweeney reeked of hatred of water. On wet days they stood in the door of the shed and hurt with bitter words.

'Tá Cormac gan athair: tá Cormac gan athair,' 'Cormac has no father' would drone from their vile mouths on days they picked on me.

The reshaped shoe scorched its print into the hoof.

In the raw smell of the smoke the hoof became a foot, Tinker's, Bolg's. 'Cormac is *gan athair*' . . . Hisss!, and hisss, as I went around each hoof. And somewhere in the swirling smoke Squire Wallace waited.

Grandpa offered me the reins to guide the pony to the Glens. 'The old hands are giving in to the neglect of the years but they're great for a weather forecast!' he observed as he showed me the swollen knuckles. 'And how're you getting on at school, young Cormac?' he enquired.

'Grand with the master; we get on fine. If you hear of a fiddle going cheap, yourself and Granma might come together on it for me.'

'Ah well, 'tis great to see a lad happy at school.'

I didn't respond, at least not in words. The pony clip-clopped over the county bounds. Granma made eye signals across to him. He tried again.

She drew her shawl over her head against the piercing wind and brought the flour-sack with its two cakes of bread underneath the shawl.

'There would never be fights at school now like there used to be in my time, I suppose?'

'You mean like faction fights; lads from one district ganging up against another?'

'Or lads making trouble for one another?'

'We have that all right, a few looking for trouble and the rest afraid to stop them for fear of what would happen to themselves.'

He didn't say anything but I knew by the tilt of his head that his ears were waiting. I continued. 'There were more of them at it in my class but I let them see what they really were. But there are still two that I haven't figured a way of handling, yet.'

'Boys, too, are they?'

'Pigs more likely; and bad mannered too.'

'Some of the girls were worse in my time.'

Granma Healy moved to say something but Granpa read her meaning in her eyes. 'Do your mother and father know about these buckos?' Granpa's eyes searched me.

'Mammy doesn't; Brad would have an idea because we talked in general one night.'

'And what did he say?' Granma asked.

'He said not to expect him to fight my battles for me and to think about the fox and how he can make a pack of hounds look foolish.'

Their eyes weighed up each other's reaction across the trap. They didn't see me looking. Jack Frost on the northeasterly could not chill the warmth lingering in their exchange of glances.

Brad couldn't settle in the kitchen or the yard. Granma fussed in and out of the new room where Nurse Relihan was attending to Mammy. At an eye-signal from Brad I took Laurie out to the cowstall, where we were soon joined by Granpa. I wanted to be alone in the old room where Granny Rua died the last time this happened. Laurie and Polka played in the hay so I climbed half way up the ladder. Granpa settled himself on the lower rungs. He too was watching Laurie and Polka but I doubt if he was thinking the thoughts they brought to me.

Granny Rua had thought a girl would be nice before Laurie was born but she just missed seeing my wishes come true. What if it were to be a girl this time? Why not! Not all girls were like Snotty Higgins or Betsy Foran. In fact the way we were growing up she would more likely turn out like Mags-the-well or Margaret Wally, angels in the company of their mothers but mischievous funny little devils at school, or anywhere together. Yes, a sister like those or indeed like cousin Breda would be grand. Of course if she was like Mammy . . . but no need to be greedy, as Mammy herself might say.

The birth of my sister, Niamh, and Uncle Peter's and Breda's wedding took place under the shadow of Tinker Burke's and Bolg Sweeney's increasing tyranny over my life at school. Their unchecked intimidation had sunk to picking on girls as well. It was during a particularly sickening incident when Bolg pulled the bottom of Betsy's dress over her head while Tinker pulled down her pants that I forgot Brad's advice never to retaliate.

It made Betsy a friend for life but the knee into Tinker's guts and the blood I drew from Bolg's nose brought even more unwelcome attention my way. Tinker and Bolg described in detail the parts of me they would remove and how they would spend a whole weekend killing me.

Now I could really feel the grip that must have tightened in my father's stomach and throat as he fought his killers. My blood would be drained into a bucket whilst I was still alive, later to be made into black puddings. What was left, bones and all, would be fed to Tinker's hungry mongrels. There wouldn't be a trace of me left but that didn't matter; I was only a bastard, they said, a bastard afraid to fight.

As neither Tinker nor Bolg copied my sums, I had to figure another way of leading them into trouble. I wouldn't be happy starting secondary school in the autumn leaving them with the satisfaction of having got the better of me. That was not the MacRua way.

FIVE

The music with the master was like warm honey on a sore throat. In the old fiddle Granpa bought I could find serenity from any storm. The master showed me how to play a tune with the expression Granny Rua used to put into a song. He wondered why I would sometimes hang as if I was astray in the movement of a tune or lose my way in reciting a poem. Brad didn't have to wonder.

'You're picking a right good time to be sharp with your brother, after young Niamh shoving him out of the nest.'

I hadn't thought about it like that: others feeling the edge of my hurt. The pang that I might squeeze fear into my young brother Laurie like Tinker and Bolg pained in me, made me feel sick. 'Sorry. I'll try not to do it again. But he can be annoying at times.'

'What do you expect? He's only a child.'

A flash of lightning quickly followed by the sharp cracking of thunder put my troubles in proportion.

'We're going down to that white hole in the Owmore, to where you spotted the trap that time but we're going for a reason. Tonight is ideal; they won't be out in weather like this.'

'You mentioned that I could feel a fish under the water when I was fourteen. Sure I was that a month ago.'

'The time wasn't right; tonight is. So stop thinking about yourself and train your senses on your surroundings. Gather your mind to what you're supposed to be doing. Tonight is your test.'

The sally branches tickled the swirling waters at the far side.

Foam perched there as on an agitated pint of stout in the night. This was where I had envisaged the giant of Hare Mountain washing his feet.

'They're not in there surely? We couldn't get near them there?'

'They bask in there sometimes; we'll come to that and something else in a minute. Now just up here, under the overhang of the reeds and rushes, the hens face the quieter flow of the water. This is where you'll shake hands with your first one.'

He lowered himself into the rushes on the shelf just above the water and eased in his left hand. I squatted between the bushes on the bank looking down at him.

Soon it was my turn. We switched places. I hoped one of those flashes of lightning wouldn't stray our way.

'Just leave your hand dangle in the water nice and loose. If something rubs against it just leave it. You can tell me as it happens.' I dangled my hand and waited. All I could feel was the coldness of the water and a pain squeezing around the bone.

'There's one there now, nibbling on my small finger.'

'Good; feel the beak.'

'It's a hen; and there's another one rubbing off me.'

'Good. Now caress it, like you did with the back of Niamh's neck the other night when she went to sleep on your shoulder. Nice light touches and it'll keep coming back for more. Touch, don't squeeze.'

'There's a third one, I'm sure, a bigger one.'

'Right, see how he reacts to the same thing.'

'He's wriggling, and he's nibbling at my fingers too. Ouch!'

'Out you come: I think you'll find you're bleeding.'

He was right. In the chill of the water I didn't feel the skin being broken. I was wishing this new intercourse with nature could go on for ever.

'I suppose you know why these lads are picking on you?'

'I wish I did; then I might fox a way out of it.'

'Jealousy, envy: they can't be as clever as you, so they want to make you as rough as themselves.'

'Uncouth, the Master calls them sometimes.'

'So what are you going to do now?'

'Wouldn't it be great if they fell into that foam on top of the whirlpool?'

We moved back down on to the strand opposite the foam. Something about the whirlpool bothered him. 'Remember I told you about Ellen, your aunty you never saw, that's where she was thrown from up there on top, and the river in flood. She never had a chance, even though she was a powerful swimmer.'

He stopped speaking. Shoulders heaved; breath hissed in gasps. He gathered me to him and rubbed his tears into my hair. 'They can't be let away with this; with the murder of your father, and my father and my sister.'

'I know, Brad.'

'If I fail you'll carry it through: you must.'

'I know: sure that's what my dad was trying to do.'

We returned to the job on hand, to the prospect of bullies in the whirlpool.

'Better lads than them failed to get out of that pool; but there's other ways of hooking your fish. I helped your father with a plan when we were in a situation like yours, only we were a bit older at the time.'

'What did ye do?'

The thunder, as if realising it was intruding in a sacred moment, rumbled off beyond the Glens.

'It was his idea mostly. A cunning genius he was, in a tight corner; until that last one, whatever happened.

'Five of them there were altogether, two lots of brothers, a three and a two from Hare Mountain. Kept annoying us to show them how to catch a salmon. He drove them mad; wouldn't even answer them, only burned holes through them with his eyes. They couldn't take it, and, well – you know all about what can happen then. So this was the spot he chose to set them up.'

'So now ye've caught me but I'll bet neither of you ever caught a salmon.'

They released me as if I had come out of uncle Danny's fire. 'A salmon! Did you ever catch a salmon?'

'Of course he did! Isn't it well known about all his crowd?' Tinker swaggered with his knowledge.

'Show us how to catch a salmon and you can be our best friend.' Bolg's eyes awed as wide as his mouth.

'I've never asked you a favour before, have I, Betsy?'

'I was hoping you would, Cormac.'

'Only if you can keep a secret; you mustn't tell *anybody*.'

'Oh, I'm going to love this; what do you want me to do? I owe you big.'

'There are five or six beautiful salmon, the size of your leg every one of them. And they're in the white hole in Owmore river, straight down from Highgrove Manor.'

'Why are you telling me that?'

'Because Brad promised to show me how to catch one tonight.'

'He's going to show you how to catch a salmon! Really?'

'Isn't it exciting. I'll tell you all about it tomorrow.'

'You're my best friend, Cormac MacRua. Oh, tomorrow; I can't wait.'

The master played the polka along with me for the first time that evening, tempo dancing in his bow, music dancing in his eyes. The surging vitality, the freedom in the music lifted me into the night's work.

They were a furlong below us in the fog, Bolg, Tinker and two others Brad identified as having the bluster of their fathers. Their noises made it difficult to sense other intrusions into the rhythm of the night. Brad squeezed my elbow. We both picked up the sounds of Rex and his accompanying terrier, downstream. That was my cue for diversion.

I stole quickly on to the bank upstream and lobbed two rocks into the river as a signal for our *poachers* to spring into action after a gap of half a minute. The rocks splashed into the whirlpool as I ran to Brad. When I turned for a look, two bogdeal torches were illuminating the fog. I had to run to stay with his half- trot back up through the forest, home to the Glens.

That was the summer of the scythe. It was the summer of change in Heather Hill and the Glens. It was the summer when Mammy showed the power inside her gentleness. The humid April followed by a wet and windy May painted the truth of the old proverb on the high craggy meadows. They showed off their glistening greenery to the elements which had coaxed their lustre from the forbidding fertility beneath.

The four weeks from mid-June to mid-July were hay-cutting and saving time. The man whose hay was still standing for Killarney races was regarded as an agricultural joke. The new horsedrawn mowing machines were fine on level or gently sloping fields. Only the scythe could master the high glens. Up here the few level fertile fields won from the wild tended to be used as gardens. The scythemen came from the Connors, the Cronins and the MacRuas.

Johnsey Connor was stretched on a board after over-reaching to a somersault off the steepest part of his own cliffs. Butty Cronin, even with the liberal use of goosegrease and poteen, couldn't supple himself out of the winter rheumatics.

Brad shod a new scythe and set the *duirníní* for my grip and posture. I had learned the rhythm of the swing and the deftness of the finish with the spare scythe when helping him to clean the lower slopes at Easter.

It was an early summer Friday when Brad announced during the supper that we'd be mowing Flemings' cliffs starting at dawn so as to get a day's work in before the sun dried away the moisture.

'He's a bit young, isn't he?' said Mammy. 'What's wrong with the Flemings themselves or the other men around here?'

'They can't edge and if you can't edge you can't get the right cut and you'll end up with a butchered sward.'

'When did Cormac learn how to edge?'

'He's still learning. His father and myself started in them cliffs when we were his age. He won't learn any younger.'

Any time Mammy argued with Brad about me he would win her silence by what my father had done. Yet there was a warning in her look that ensured my first day's edge was regularly checked. He confined me to a sward little more than half the width of his rhythmic strokes setting the pace ahead of me. We got home that evening about the same time as Granma Healy's unexpected arrival.

Brad went off to busy himself in the garden field, accompanied by Laurie and the dogs. I immersed my stinging hands in the soothing water of the barrel in the yard as Granpa set out on his journey home to Heather Hill.

'I don't mind her coming into my kitchen but I'll not abide her getting into my oven.'

'You must be taking her up wrong, Mother. Breda isn't like that.'

'You live with her and you'll see what she's like. Completely

72

taken over the place, she has.'

'She is the woman of the house, you know. What did you do when you married in there?'

'That was different. The old woman was delighted to have me around so she could go off and visit the neighbours and play her concertina or talk to her rosary when she got the notion.'

'So my grandmother allowed you to take over the place, like you say Breda is doing now?'

'I'd expect more sympathy from my own daughter.'

'You're forgetting how you implored me not to leave you with no one to take my place. Well, you have her now.'

'I have her now is right. No shred of sympathy left in the world any more.'

I imagined Granma chopping the air with her hands as she signed her words, which she still did when upset. I was about to go back inside when Mammy's considered words brought a new dimension to the problem.

'Now that you're here you're welcome to my oven and pots.'

'Ah, sure I knew you had a heart. What do you want done?'

'I have a husband and two sons that would eat the table if there wasn't enough on it. That's what I want done, for the next week: keep my table.'

'Only for a week?'

'And then you can go home to Breda. If you're still short of a job you could get Danny to do the decent thing with the woman that's waiting for him.'

An acre a day on level friendly ground was regarded as good mowing for a scytheman. Brad and I were doing two acres between us. Brad trebled my work in a race with time. It was thirsty work but homebrewed cider and a mixture of milk and water stored in the cool shade of the dykes gave us something to race to the headland for in alternate swards. It was as if Brad had nettles in his trousers at such a rest-period near the end of a day's work when he found words for a delicate subject.

'Your little sister Niamh is a lovely child, isn't she?'

'Oh, a pure little pet and she's getting so clever.'

'You'd want to be careful you don't spoil her, now. She's very fond of you altogether.'

''Twould be hard to turn my back on her.'

'Of course you know where children come from?'

'Yes, I do. I figured that out a good while ago.'

'And how they happen to be – conceived?'

'Conceived?'

'Yes, how they find themselves starting out in their mother's tummies.'

'Well, it must be something like the male and female animals.'

'A bit like that, yes, but different for people. It seals their relationship with each other for life.'

'The catechism at school says 'tis a sin except in marriage.'

'I was wondering when you were going to get around to that. You're asking me how you came about?'

'Well, I know that much – through Mammy and Dad. Does that mean my father died in sin and is burning in hell?'

He was silent. The moment shivered in the heat of the sun. Our swards of newmown hay glistened in the waiting. 'Was it a priest told you that?'

'No, 'tis in the catechism.'

'There's also something in there about God's mercy, and love, and understanding. If your father is gone to hell then heaven must be an awful lonesome place altogether.'

I didn't reply; he didn't seem to expect one. We returned to our mowing in silence, carrying my father in the rhythm of our thoughts.

As well as the heavy work mowing from dawn to noon, Brad also sprayed some of the local potato gardens from a knapsack, a copper container strapped to his back. It held about five gallons of a mixture of bluestone and washing-soda pumped out to a spray through handheld nozzles. What was left of him when he came home on those evenings had me wondering how he got home at all. Mother would hide her concern as she gave him a hot wash out of the zinc bath, saw that he ate a good supper before he lay on the bed for a massage of a mixture of goose grease and poteen. He was always asleep before she finished, and sometimes I noticed tears dropping on to the shiny skin as she kneaded away the pain of his day.

One Saturday I also had to join in with a knapsack as sultry mists threatened to bring blight to the Glens. Brad showed me how to aim the spray through the nozzles to ensure good cover for the stalks against the blight. He explained how the blight could get into a garden through a gap in a ditch, leaving its black death in a path through the stalks. I learned that the widespread blight which caused the great famine of 1847 had its roots in lesser blights over the previous few years resulting in stunted crops yielding seed potatoes which were themselves blight-infected.

The home we plodded back to between dusk and dark had a tightness in the air like that day in Millstreet before Mammy's wedding.

'A great place, surely, the Glens. Sure the MacRuas are always there to mow your hay and spray your spuds and catch your game,' she said.

Brad hid his hurt in the shadows of his dark sockets in the lamplight.

'Men they call themselves around here is it, Brad MacRua? Men! Not many of them are men unless they have a glass in their hands, as far as I can see.'

Brad couldn't argue with that, and didn't.

'And they must be rightly pleased that the new generation is ready at their service. Sweet suffering Christ, there must be awful activity in their grave down there in Benmore if himself and old Brad can see the slavery, the same old pattern of drudgery repeating itself.'

Laurie peeped out from the loft as she fell into a chair in tears, bringing Brad out of his stool to hold her to him whispering 'Deirdre, Deirdre, Deirdre.'

Her fury vented, she quickly composed herself and set about massaging the day out of Brad while I was to give myself a hot overall wash in readiness for the same. Under the gentle power of her hands my aches gave way to a soothing reverie. As her fingers found the depths of my body she reminded me that there was more to life than being a slave to drudgery, even if that slavery earned local adulation. She talked of my father. He would have done this work, as Brad said, but only to help out.

My father's dream must be carried on, his vision of the best in local tradition taken into a bigger world, blended and improved through contact with other traditions. He would encourage hard work but only if it didn't fetter me from getting out into that world beyond the Glens. She seemed to know my father better than Brad knew his twin.

The master had brought me to a stage where I could play any tune by ear by my fourteenth birthday. The fun, the magic I had looked forward to in that birthday, could only probe an occasional beam through the gathering clouds. Wishing to be big found me wishing to be bigger. Fourteen at fourteen was just another rocky field compared to the lustre fourteen seemed to hold at thirteen.

Mother again found an ally in the master in supporting her views of my future against those of Brad. These three people I loved were turning against each other because of me. Or was I wrong?

Perhaps it was because of their image of the man I should become to meet their vision of a community's winning back ownership of its fish and game. My father, who had sown the seed of such thinking, was silenced. Was I expected to bring in the new harvest? What did this mean? What kind of crop would this be? Would there be blood on the blade I would use to reap it? My father: a sharpening silhouette from the past about to determine my future. And from within, my own dreams of prospects in future horizons. Me: yearning for the company of the man who would signpost my goals; my convenient proxy to making some of my own decisions. I avoided him in my tantalising web of feelings towards Mags-the-well and Margaret Wally.

Brad: what was he trying to do? Was he doing what he was thinking? The more I teased the conflict between his actions and his words, the more convinced I became that he, perhaps even more than I, was missing his half-twin.

Like Brad I was left-handed so it was easy to imitate his actions in preparing for the real catch, not to be attempted until I had completed the specified set-up. I was toughened from manual work and from bouts of racing up the Glens with Loopy and Polka. He still considered that my arms and shoulders needed conditioning, despite the sometimes heavy work with Uncle Danny in the forge. My race up the Glens was reduced to a trot as I gripped a rock in each hand through barriers of pain and fatigue. And as I mastered my grip on one pair of rocks a heavier and more awkward pair were introduced. Soon he could see that I would endure anything to be ready to complete a catch, including chin-ups on any tree in the forest, arm wrestling with Brad himself and hauling on that weight-laden rope he had used for his own tug-of-war training. Time was running out. If he knew that I intended starting in secondary school after the holidays ended in two weeks, he would not have schooled me for the catch. Mother on the other hand had enrolled me in the school, and was making the necessary preparations.

The night he chose was a wet howler but with reasonable visibility in a more inaccessible section of the river than we had spotted in daylight beforehand. Loopy and Polka were also with us, both now responsive to the most subtle signals of whistle and whisper. I lay among the reeds and rushes and eased my left arm into the dark chilly water. Brad squatted just above me in the briars. He sensed the tangle of my excitement, and rubbed my head.

'Gather your mind to what you're at; you'll do grand.' The dogs lay heads-in-paws out of view. For what seemed like ages there was nothing. Brad reminded me to let the arm hang there and wait. Patience would bring me the company I was waiting for. It came initially in the anticipated rubbing just above the wrist and then fitting the beak into my hand. Brad knew by my reaction that nature was taking its course.

'The beak. Don't forget the beak,' he whispered as my index finger felt the jutting spike of the cock. The more playful hen was now joining in the fun and I began to feel those differences Brad had described.

The hen wriggled through my scratching fingers like a fun-loving cat. The more static cock followed. I waited until he turned against the flow of the river. His breathing fins opened; my fingers dug in, and then he was out among the briars on the bank. Brad didn't move. Two notes of a subtle whistle bade the dogs to stay as the cock threshed about in the briars. Then I saw the lights two furlongs away where we had been spotting openly for the previous few days.

'Right, go to it now!' Brad ordered.

In a quick movement I brought back the top of his beak; my salmon quivered to stillness. The dogs crawled into position in response to Brad's whistle. I balanced the salmon between Loopy's jaws.

'Fetch home! Fetch home and wait! Upward, upward, down and even-slow,' went Brad's quiet whistle. Loopy and Polka slipped homewards through the night.

We stole through the protection of the briars and bushes into the forest that would cover our way home. In a well-used cattle gap overlooking the lights searching that section of the river, I rubbed my hands in the mud to get rid of the scales. On our way through the forest I probed Brad's shell. 'Do you still miss your brother?'

''Twould save a lot of trouble if he was around these times anyway.'

'Even though you argued about things.'

'You're turning out the same way as him. Education! See where it got him.' I had to run to catch up with him. 'There's more to the making of a man than poking himself out into the world or probing books and history of people that have nothing at all to do with our way of life.'

'So he'd see things Mother's way if he was around?'

'And the master's; but you had better do a bit of thinking for yourself. People around here don't like to see folks getting above themselves.' He paused.

'You're doing grand now the way you are, getting respect for what you are able to do instead of who you are.'

'My father was well respected, like you?'

'People expect a MacRua to carry through the gains of previous generations. Your father was more than willing.'

My father, more than willing: what of the son?

'Your mother is right when she talks that way about him.' He turned his eyes towards Highgrove Manor and back to me again, blinking.

'He was in a frightful hurry: I wish I knew why he chose that night to put things right without telling me.'

He stopped again. My father was losing his lustre.

'So he was wrong! Is that what you're saying?'

'Other people sat back and made balls for him to fire. He wasn't wrong, blinded maybe by other wrongs, the basic issues of gaming and fishing rights.'

He walked on. I followed. The basic issues waited, unresolved. If they were as simple as they appeared to Brad and as important as everybody said, what was the delay? Why was my father dead or were those issues also dying?

'I'm going to stay on at school, Brad; there are things I have to figure out.'

Loopy and Polka waited. Brad carried a brooding silence before me into the smokehouse.

The bicycle Mother had bought for me was a little too big, but I would be growing into it. She made the long trousers I had to wear to secondary school, a restricting garment I could only accept after I saw the other boys in similar garb. Against Mother's advice I reacted violently to the practice of 'baptising' first year students in the school. One boy lost a tooth, another suffered cracked ribs and a third ended up like myself with a pair of black eyes. This was good. I was sorry I hadn't settled the score in national school as I had begun in secondary. Now I was aware that Brad's conditioning programme had prepared me for other battles, apart from catching salmon. Attack the weakness of the attackers; yes, this surely was the way.

Next day the parents of the ribs arrived at the school to demand that the principal make an example of the bully who so brutally attacked and injured their angelic offspring. Headmaster saved the situation by insisting that the boy tell the whole story. Later, on my own, he warned me that if I wasn't to make life a misery for myself and everybody around me I would have to learn to control my temper. For emphasis he put me on notice that my future in the school depended on that control.

SIX

Reillys' rambling house was a long thatched cabin halfway between our house and Benmore village. The first time I saw one of those holiday postcards caricaturing the large plump lady and her beanpole husband I saw Nancy and Dandy Reilly, a couple whose ages were suspended somewhere in their late sixties. They ensured that all the inherited conventions of this third-generation rambling house were observed. Girls under eighteen could not attend unless accompanied by an older family member. Fathers of young families were not welcome without their wives, thus ensuring that adequate arrangements were made to look after the children in their absence, usually by the grandparents or other extended family members.

The rambling house was out of bounds for girls and boys under fifteen but they were expected to attend to signify their transition from childhood to individuality in their own right as soon as possible after their fifteenth birthday, the boys unaccompanied, the girls accompanied on that first occasion by their mothers or older sisters.

That Friday night after my birthday on 15 February 1954 saw the beginning of the end of a nasty convention. Mother fussed over me. She checked again that my first long pants she had made from a worn-out pair of Brad's fitted me properly along with the new *báinín* jumper and hobnailed boots.

Brad waited at the edge of the yard with advice not to be afraid to dance as Mother had taught me and to keep my head in case of any horseplay. When I queried the horseplay he just repeated that I shouldn't take too much notice of any silly fooling among the lads.

I noticed Mags-the-well, also on her first night, tucked in beside her mother in the warmth of the Reillys' welcome. A reputation as a fiddler student of the master had preceded me. Dandy put it to the test with a request for a few tunes so that Nancy and himself could have an early dance before taking over the playing. Dandy's fiddle coated with years of resin dust and soot responded with a full-bodied resonance to the bow.

Three fairy-reel sets soon formed. I marvelled at those hobnailed boots keeping their balance, bouncing and turning on flagstones polished from generations of dancing. Two of the men, long Tom Flood and Bill Daly, had their own ways of negotiating the dance. Tall clumsy Tom crouched, backside jutting out for balance, performing the dance steps a fraction later than the others. Bill Daly, with a reputation for being fond of the women, tried to impress, gripping his tongue between his teeth to get through the more complicated movements. Nearing the end of the set, I noticed Mags was the only one not dancing. Her long chestnut hair bobbed in a tartan ribbon to the beat. Her eyes betrayed the mischievous look which usually signalled the hatching of a plot between herself and Margaret Wally. She was teasing him.

The little devil was daring Bill on to even more fancy footwork, taunting him with that unspoken language. Something about her demeanour reminded me of a luscious ripe apple tantalisingly out of reach in the topmost branch of a tree. The apple wanted to be reached but the tree was her mother.

The master brought the soul of each piece of music to life under his fingers. He had taught me how to put vitality into a dance tune, not by playing a faster tempo but by putting expression into the rhythm; the dancer would then find more bounce without really trying. And these dancers were bouncing. Nancy insisted that I play a slow air while everybody took a rest. In my lessons with the master I had played the dance music while seated. I found that I got more feeling and embellishment into the slow airs while standing, my eyes closed for improved concentration.

I went into 'She Moved through the Fair', starting out to tease Mags, but what I was getting from Dandy's fiddle soon closed my eyes and thoughts to everybody. A surge of feelings like those I experienced when encountering danger with Brad or with Uncle Danny in the forge welled up to my fingertips as the sensation of the power of the music became part of me. I was a young boy seated in Granny Rua's lap as she sang to the faded brown picture of herself and old Brad, my thoughts and images perched on the way she held her notes and expression.

Two groups of eight took the floor for the polka set which followed. Dandy on the fiddle was accompanied by Nancy on the concertina. I joined one of the sets with Mags, opposite her mother partnered by the shuffling figure of Tom Flood. Tom was a bachelor farmer in his sixties. It was rumoured that the matchmaker had found a young woman named Moll who was to marry Tom next Shrove. I wondered at what kind of woman would fall in love with that gangling figure of well over six feet with no neck and exceptionally long legs. His backside seemed to jut out even more for the dancing of the polka and there was definitely a delay in messages *en route* from his ears to those size twelve feet. A snot occasionally tried to escape from his nose. He would allow it to dangle over a landing spot for a few seconds before taking it by surprise, snorting it back to base and spitting it into the fire.

Though her partner's movements were frequently unco-ordinated, and he too had to grip his tongue between his teeth for the more difficult parts, Mags' mother was obviously enjoying her dance. It was while I was thinking of how my mother would enjoy and deserve such an occasion that Mags gave my hand a squeeze to remind me that it was our turn to lead on the *show-off* movement. While the other couples watched us, I became aware of comments from the men that I could be flighty, hard to handle and might even best them like the two before me.

The last and longest movement of the polka was the hornpipe involving four changes of partner. I remember being surprised at how light Mags' mother was on her feet for such a big woman, and how easily I could control her in a swing.

At the end of the dance I was grabbed from behind. Bill and Dandy tried to get hold of my legs. I kicked them away, catching Bill on the jaw and dazing him. Another took his place, so I had to repeat. I then realised it was Tom Flood who was holding me from behind. I got an elbow back hard enough assisted by the heel of my boot on the shin to double him up where we had been dancing. The crowd formed a ring around us, goaded by Nancy. I was thankful that Mother had insisted I wear my new hobnailed boots; they soon lost interest in trying to grab my legs. In a rage I roared that the next man to touch me would need the priest and doctor.

Mags was sobbing in her mother's arms. I charged for the door and ran back up the Glens, followed briefly by Dandy shouting that it was all meant as a bit of fun.

Brad's fine-tuned ear had heard me coming, waiting with Mother at the door. She dabbed at the blood round my mouth and over my right eye.

'An old ritual that must go back to pagan times,' Brad said. My temper wasn't helped by the realisation that Brad had known what I was walking into. I calmed down under Mother's gentle hands. Brad explained that the fifteen-year-old boy would be grabbed and his pubic area inspected to see if hairs were sprouting as signs of manhood.

An earlier remark of the night fell into place. I asked if the same had happened to him and my father.

'They tried it on the two of us together but they didn't have a hope. Now that it has failed with you it'll probably die out, and not before its time.' I was glad to hear Brad accepting that a tradition had outlived its relevance.

Horse-drawn machinery brought a new age to the Glens. While Brad reluctantly acknowledged the transition, it was Mother who analysed the problem by referring to previous summers when Brad and I had taken up the work abandoned by generations who had followed the lure of a better life beyond the Irish Sea or the Atlantic. While the traditional way of doing things had to adapt to whoever was available to do them, tradition itself ordained that each small farmer tilled his garden, sowed and reaped his crops and saved his hay and corn.

Tradition had taken the Brad MacRua of each generation hostage as its leader, although at a price. The cost this time was a new type of debt. A plough with interchangeable single and double boards, a mowing machine and a spraying machine, all horsedrawn, were purchased in Ballybo. The arrangements for financing the machinery brought Mother and Brad to the bank. The operation of the machinery made it into a business for which Brad was ill-prepared.

Mother had grown up in a house where books were figured for the trades of stonemason and blacksmith, so she recognised exactly what had to be done. Brad had been reared in a barter system: the idea of charging money for ploughing or mowing or spraying was anathema. A new and cruel reality emerged as the date of the first repayment to the bank was followed by the second and the strain leading to the third, putting a frost on the silence between Mother and Brad. Yet Brad hadn't mentioned money or bills to any of his eager customers. They were all neighbours for whom he had done the winter and spring ploughing, sowing and planting, and he could not think of them in the commercial terminology of customers. He hid his reluctance in excuses.

Even though he had ploughed, harrowed, drilled and sowed the crops, the job would not be done until the harvest was brought in, he said. The tension snapped on Mother's silence. Brad was being taken advantage of yet again and he was too busy or too blind to recognise it. Her anger with Brad's forbearance lost patience with his customers' presumptions.

Laurie and Niamh took the immediate impact. Their shock was one of disbelief that Mother had such an opposite side to her protectiveness. I at least had caught the increasingly oppressive scent for days beforehand and took my blame for not having costed the jobs or agreed unit prices on an hourly, daily, area or quantity basis.

The pallor of Mother's skin was taut over the fine structure of her face as she accused Brad of having a bag of sentimental curds in place of guts. She must have noticed the shock of his crushed reaction and tried to soften the impact by calling him a busy fool as he escaped into the peace of the night.

By midnight two unused halves of my copy books had become indexed and numbered pages of a ledger telling names, addresses, dates, particulars and amounts due for work done. I calculated the amounts. Mother debited the value of completed work to the individual accounts, while on the right hand side of each sheet she ruled off the credit columns. All but two, who had made payments on account, were blank on the credit side. It was clear that the value of work to date would clear our commitments for the year with money to spare.

That account with the squire came to mind: credit side blank: debit side written in blood. To balance brought down, three MacRua lives. Just how would this account be balanced? Mother's voice pulled me back.

'Stepper could do with a rest. We haven't charged for her at all and she nearly killed from the drag of work. I bet their horses are looking at her with a shine on them from the fat.'

'I don't know, Mother, will they ever pay?'

'They mightn't plan to pay Brad; but there are many ways of separating the genuine from the chancer.'

It was three in the morning when she asked me to look for him. He hadn't returned to the house since his heavyhearted departure under Mother's bitter words. She had drifted in and out of sleep but her face showed that she could wait no longer. My mother inside, layered with worry; Brad out there somewhere laden with other people's burdens, and with the-Lord-only-knew-what locked up in his heart. Had he cracked? If he were sent to look for himself at this time of night, where would he start? Did he want to be found? Would he resent my intrusion into the insides of his night? The dogs, especially Loopy, would know. Find Loopy and I would find Brad. My whistle for Loopy brought Polka to my side; my next whistle brought Loopy's bark from the byre, signifying his loyalty to a prior duty.

I could sense his troubled presence as I adjusted to the darkness. He sat leaning back against the ladder leading to the hay loft. Loopy squatted on his behind, facing Brad. I waited for him to speak but I soon felt that I was unwelcome.

'Mother is wondering where you are.'

'Is she now? Wondering where I am, indeed! Well now you can tell her where I am.'

'Aren't you coming in? It's very late.' I wondered whether I should manoeuvre around or through his silence.

'Mother is very worried; it's not a bit fair, the way she is.'

'So the scholar is trying to tell me how to look after his mother now, is he! Do you hear that, Loopy? Our genius that's going to change the way of doing things in the Glens wants me to mind his mother for him.'

I wanted to tell him that I could look after my own mother, that she was his wife, expecting his third child, and her fourth, very soon by the looks of her. I wanted to tell him – what was the use? I now felt what it must have been like for Granma Healy before her tongue was loosened – things she was bursting to say but her mouth not knowing what to do.

I coaxed my legs to take me back inside the house. As I closed the door, two strong beams of light from the forest searched the front of the house and yard and swept back again in case they had missed anything.

'Where is he? In the name of God, what's that light?'

'He's out in the byre talking to his dog and is in no mood to come in. I think we should all go back to bed.'

'Is he all right?'

'He's not worried whether you're all right, so I don't see why you should be worried. Do you want me to stay downstairs for what's left of the night?'

'That would help, if you don't mind.'

'I'll sleep with you if you like.'

'Oh, Cormac, I don't know: I don't think that would be a good idea any more. You're too young to understand these things.'

Granny Rua's old bed still creaked as I tried to settle myself between Mother's and Brad's situation.

He out there in the byre in a mood that excluded both of us; she below in her bed wanting me near but not too near. And what was I too young to understand? This situation between Brad and herself? And why in the course of half a night should my feelings have turned against Brad? Once again I wished I could speak to my father.

Next morning I was tackling Stepper under the trap when Brad challenged me. 'Where do you think you're going with the trap, and a load of work to be done?'

'Mother wants the trap for very important business of her own. Whoever wants the machinery can provide their own horses.'

'What's this important business you're talking about?'

'I have a good idea but I'm only guessing. Ask her yourself if you want to know.'

'I'm asking you.'

'If you're that interested you can ask herself.'

I hopped into the trap and trotted Stepper around to the door to escape the dark rings of his glare.

Mother chewed up excuses and spat them gently back at their source. Some were profuse with their apologies for bringing a woman in her condition to their doors to collect what was her due. Others had to have their attitudes adjusted.

'So you expect people to be at your service free of charge?'

'Well no, Mam, 'tis, I mean . . . '

'Or maybe you can't afford it, though I can't see what you spend the money on?'

'Oh I can pay my way, only I don't know why he had to send a messenger.'

'Because he's too busy working for the likes of you too ready to take advantage of him.'

Mother's demeanour was the precise definition of contempt. She watched the ape-mouth open and close. He scratched his backside with one hand and his dirty pate with the other trying to squirm his way out of this unaccustomed difficulty. 'I said two pounds seven shillings and sixpence and if you waste any more of my time it'll be two pounds ten.'

Snake Mohan peeled a five pound note from a bundle and scratched himself again while she counted his change.

It was a race to get to town before the bank closed. I didn't like the look on her face as she recovered from the stench of eyeballing the Snake. But the pledge on her word compelled her to meet the family commitment to the manager as the proceeds of our sweat eroded our debt.

Busy: shopping in Ballybo, tidying the house, stocking up fuel for the fire, filling the pots over the fire with water after we came home. Brad still in self-imposed exile in the byre.

Mother roused me out of Granny's old bed: get the fire going well, plenty of water, the pot, the kettle. No time to go for the nurse. No need. I would help. Cormac would help his mother, wouldn't he?

'Should I get Brad from the byre?'

'No, not now. Let him be. Anyway he claims to sense these things.'

Towels, balls of cottonwool, water, hot and cold. She bites that cold towel again as I dab her brow, sharp fast breaths. Sheet kicked off revealing the swollen tummy, the thighs, layers of sacking under her.

'Wet your fingers. Go around inside and ease out the head when I push.'

A push, another, still more. Poor Mammy; I must try to do more. A muffled scream into a bitten towel, slimy head.

'Support the head – help me.' A heaving push, more, more. 'Take it. Lift it up. Out . . . '

Everything so slippery. She takes it from me, her deft hands to their instinctive task. More water. I return to meet my new sister, so tiny, yet taking up so much of Mother. I make porridge out of ground oats, mixed with milk and a little salt and honey, as near to the way she likes it as I can. Laurie and Niamh peep through sleepy eyes from the loft. A baby sister: Mammy is very tired. Just a quick look and then back up to bed.

Brad at the door. Red eyes look through me and my work.

'A baby girl, while ago, just like Niamh; I was about to tell you.'

He pushes the half door behind him, leans back, hunched. I pass him down a large bowl of porridge, a jar of warm milk, and honey.

'She's expecting you anyway; maybe you should come with me.' He was back; now we were six.

Any bicycle was new in the Glens in 1955, so when Betsy Foran rode one into our yard near the end of June she created almost as much excitement as when I had helped Mother to deliver my baby sister Mary two weeks earlier. Betsy had finished her schooling after confirmation, and was now working in Highgrove Manor from where she had come with a message that Brad and his new spraying machine were required forthwith to attend to the potato garden. To Mother's consternation Brad had refused, seething at the idea of Squire Wallace dispatching the bailiff's daughter with any message to the MacRua household. Interpreting the look on Mother's face I set off across the fields and frightened Betsy into the ditch as she sped around a bend. I helped her out of the briars. I noticed a scratch reddening its way from her calf to above her bare knee.

I bade her wait while I gathered and chewed a mouthful of briar and white-thorn leaves, mint, wild parsley and dock. As I pressed the green mess along the scar she raised her skirt so that I could follow it home to the elastic on the leg of her knickers. She trembled like a rabbit just caught in a snare and when she raised the skirt over the other thigh to see if any scratch needed treatment there, I found myself wanting to explore further. I wished it was Mags-the-well's or Margaret Wally's thigh that quivered expectantly under my hands.

A corncrake just inside the ditch joined in the pulse of the monotonous chorus of its colleagues.

Thighs, female thighs changing places in my head. 'You're daydreaming again, Cormac; I hope it's about me?' Betsy was ready to remount her bicycle.

'I was just thinking about something, different things. You're all right so?'

'I suppose I have to be if you're letting me go.'

I waited for another crash as she looked back over her left and then her right shoulders. Then I remembered why I was there. 'Oh, Betsy?'

'Something you forgot, Cormac?' she returned.

'I'll do the job.'

'You'll do the job! Oh, Cormac!'

'The spraying; I'll do it later today if they send me a horse.'

'Oh, the spraying; I'll tell him. I'll see you then so.'

Heather Hill had changed. It glowed in harmony with Breda. Colours blended into each other; the uniform shade of smoked timber in the loft now bore a friendly arrangement of blue and cream. Granma Healy divided her time between both her sons' homes. She wouldn't rest, Breda remarked, until she steered Danny into marriage. Danny had so far managed to pick up the scent of the traps and remained in his bachelor state. Uncle Peter's lean contours had filled out and Granpa Healy doted over Breda and Peter's twins, Laurence and Brendan.

My news from the Glens, a baby sister Mary named after Granma Healy, Peter and Breda to be godparents, was savoured.

Brad and Mother fitted easily with each other in the house when I got home. Niamh had bedded her special rag doll in with Mary and had become very possessive of her only sister. Laurie was annoyed that I hadn't taken him to Heather Hill to see the twins and Uncle Peter. He softened when I explained what Uncle Danny had done to Stepper's hooves, running around the yard with joy after I allowed him to feel each one. But Brad was different with me, giving me a feeling like the previous summer when I tried to mow a broader sward than I was comfortable with. I didn't like this difference.

A new world was opening up for me: secondary school in Ballybo was even better than I had expected; success and new friends outside the parish with the Benmore football team and athletic club; the fulfilment of playing music with the master and his friends; the thrill of being near girls. There was an excitement about Mags-the-well, Margaret Wally, and, in a different way, Betsy Foran and the situations she would get herself into so that I could 'rescue' or 'heal' her. I wished I could get that close to Mags or Margaret.

There was the spectacular world of the night, the forest, the rivers and waterfalls to which Brad had introduced me, and now it was Laurie's turn. There were many experiences I could share with Mother but I needed Brad to react with me in place of my father.

Mother and I had created the distance and Brad had drawn Laurie into it. Laurie his own son, leaving me to my apparent independence.

SEVEN

School reduced Ballybo to a smaller town in a world which was expanding through Shakespeare, Milton, Keats, Coleridge, Homer, Euclid, Pythagoras, and the goings on of Cicero, Caesar *et al* in Gaul and all along the Mediterranean. My fascination with the deeds of warriors in history such as Ghengis Khan and Ben Hur was matched only by my disgust at atrocities such as feeding Christians to the lions in the Coliseum.

Christians to the lions: MacRuas to Squire Wallace's Highgrove Manor; Spartans at war with Athenians. Surely in these mazes of hate I would find a way to transfer MacRua pain to Squire and his kin.

Mother confirmed that my father too had delved into history even to the extent of writing to libraries and universities in Belfast, Edinburgh and London to get different versions of the same events.

I found another source of joy in the night, the reckless freedom of running unseen through winter fields, sometimes sprinting or walking or climbing. The birds and animals quickly accepted my movements as a normal part of their night life, as I prepared for my attack on the squire and his manor.

High up in the forest on a Friday night when Mother and Brad thought I had returned to the rambling house, I was greeted by Rex. The magical tingle was back, concentrating my senses.

I located the bailiff and what looked like a guard keeping watch on a few miles of streams from the upper Glens. I cracked a twig and two beams of light searched the night as I drew them towards the first waterfall. I watched their approach and sent the dog towards the road while I dodged between the bushes at the other side, sending the two men in different directions, the guard taking my side.

I teased him gradually upwards on to a slippery rockface where he slipped and tumbled back down, landing on the marshy edge of a good salmon run. I watched as he got up and set about cleaning himself and his lamp; then I sped back through the safe paths of the forest.

'A chase for the sake of a chase?' Brad's anger was white.

'But I didn't plan it. The sight of them there, probably waiting for us . . .'

'You didn't plan it! You didn't think! Reckless foolishness.'

'I wanted to see what they would do. I knew they hadn't a hope of catching me.'

He hesitated. I could see his anger resting. 'You're turning out just like your father.' He left a space. I filled it with a suggestion.

'So why don't you spot a good one for tonight and I'll set up a diversion.' I watched him scratching his head.

'Whistle signals so, no fancy work, no daredevil tricks – and concentrate.'

'Long for safe – short for danger.' He nodded.

'The lad I want is lording it up at Dippers Elbow.'

'I don't know why but that's where I'd expect to find them tonight.'

'At least you're holding on to the basics; I'll wait for your signal so.' He almost smiled.

The stream whispered loudly with its flush of water from the upper Glens. A white moon peeped through the clouds drifting from the southwest and watched the heavier ones sprinkle soft showers on the slopes.

A matchlight followed by the aroma of smouldering Mick McQuaid cut plug gave away the watch. From his position Brad would have been looking down on them as I furiously brought sticks of bogdeal to a smoulder. I whistle-called to Rex. A pair of torches flashed above Dippers Elbow and moved after the German shepherd. A long and two short whistles signalled to Brad what he could already see.

A furlong out of sight would have given him enough clearance but I lured them to the luxuriant sally ford two furlongs upstream where my giveaway bogdeal flame reflected off at least seven salmon. I eased my way through the sallies at the far side. A rabbit scampered from my disturbance. Nature took its course as he raced off up the Glens pursued by Rex, allowing me to move downstream but upwind from my pursuers. Their torches were dark now, waiting for the poacher to strike.

Two whistle variations among the sounds of the night left me free to find my own way home. I raced to catch him before he went to bed and found him as expected in the smokehouse.

A magnificent twenty-five pound specimen hung from the stillers, a half stone heavier than I had ever seen before. 'Biggest by a pound I ever caught.' He observed my gaping admiration through the candlelight.

'The steaks off him won't leave much room on a plate!' I observed in awe.

'Your plan was good, but they'll know 'twas you. They'll think they frightened you off.'

'Why have you the candle lighting?'

'We'll set up the smoke. We're in for a heavy night's rain, he'll take a long time.'

'Did you ever fight when you were my age?'

'Well, I told you about your father and myself at the rambling house.'

'So it was always when you were attacked, the two of you?'

'Always: never trouble trouble till trouble troubles you.'

'The headmaster warned me to watch my temper.'

'Maybe he meant something else; you're at a dangerous age – no longer a boy and not yet a man; but the man is breaking out in you very fast.'

'You mean about Mother and me? We had to do that.'

'Maybe. But 'tis one thing to move with change but another altogether to be in front leading it by the bridle. Your father would have been proud of you, that's for sure.'

'What would he think of tonight?'

'Did you spot any fish when you lit the bogdeal?'

'Seven beauties.' The thought of them renewed temptation.

'He'd want you to lie in there and pick one from under their noses. But you handled it grand.' He divided the salmon so that we could both prepare it for the smoke. 'That's twice you left them scratching themselves. They'll have some plan ready for your third attempt, you know. So you should be putting yourself in their boots and figuring out what that plan might be.'

'They'll use two positions or maybe three and use one to drive me into the other.'

'How did you figure that out?'

'It's a classic military manoeuvre repeating itself throughout history. I must lend you one of my history books to read.'

''Tis a terrible shame you never knew your father. Amazing thing, breeding.' He slowly shook his head.

The success of the night and the late hour meant his disapproval of my three spraying visits to the potato gardens of Highgrove Manor would have to wait another time. His remark to Mother that she should wash the blood off Squire's money meant that the time to vent his disapproval to me was imminent.

Highgrove nested on a low ridge commanding five hundred acres of the foothills of Hare Mountain and owning the hunting and fishing rights of the mountain and Glens.

The large bony frame of the squire, along with his Irish wolfhound counterpart from the canine kingdom, was involved in all aspects of the running of the estate where each tree, bush and briar had a purpose. Local visitors were discouraged but guests came for the two seasonal hunts, game shooting and angling. They would travel along a washed-gravel avenue sheltering in oak, sycamore, scotch fir, birch and larch. It made its way through pampered lawns boasting double orchards, tennis and croquet courts, and an unusual intermingling of strawberry and flowerbeds.

The avenue afforded a view of the southerly aspect of the front of the manor and meandered about so as to catch the impressive westerly aspects. On my first visit I gazed at the four corner towers of sandstone accentuating the support columns giving prestige to the green front door which was furnished with polished brass looking out over a double rise of five steps each. My usual approach was over the east manor bridge crossing the Owmore river and following a steep stone boreen along by the cornfields of wheat and barley into the gardens which didn't need scarecrows, as two workmen were in constant attendance.

Even the cornfields here were bigger and superior to ours, the expanse of wheat and barley a luxuriant contrast to our hilly patches of oats coaxed from indifferent sparseness.

The threshing machine would spend three days at Highgrove; then it would come to our yard to where all the oats in the Glens were brought for threshing in one day.

The squire fussed that a lad so young might not be able to control King Henry, the frisky stud provided to take the spraying machine through the two acres of plump stalks. 'I'll be fine,' I assured him, knowing that I had a new trick in addition to the poacher-power in my arms and shoulders. He observed from the edge of my vision as I steadied the stallion with my eyes and whispered soothing verse in Irish into his ear. We then set out on our successful distribution of the first tub of bluestone and washing-soda, painting the green stalks a light, protective copper blue.

The whole environment was of nature tamed at the hand of man and of servants responsive to their master's wishes. Acres of crops grew in strict formation in their brown earthen drills without competition from weeds. The gardens, much bigger than in the Glens, were bounded by clay ditches topped with a range of bushes cropped to uniformity. Only Wally's farm a little to the west bore any comparison with the clinical neatness of my surroundings; but at least Wally's hedges allowed the birds more freedom in wilder bushes.

Squire's satisfaction with the completed job was expressed in a payment which I hadn't had an opportunity to request, a payment substantially more than the extra which Mother had advised me to add.

It was after the second spraying that he invited me to the manor. In my surprise I refused but he merely asked me to be ready to go there with him next time.

Benmore Fair introduced spring and autumn to the Glens each year. The spring fair on the second Tuesday in February was alive with breeding fowl, calves, sheep, bulls, cabbage plants, eggs, seed potatoes, pigs – and suspect horses. Sellers haggled with buyers and traded insults to probe for signs of weakness in the pursuit of bargain or opportunity.

The autumn fair was held on the Tuesday after the end of September when some of the produce of the spring fair purchases would be for sale. Buyer and seller haggled.

'That your old cow, is it?'

'Well, she wouldn't be that old now.'

'No bother to count the bones in her, and where she came from.'

'A wonder you were able to find your way here at all and where you came from.'

'Is it that you want someone to take that poor beast to the boneyard for you?'

'She'll throw more calves than you have fathers before she sees a boneyard, so if you're that anxious to improve your herd you can have her for forty pounds.'

A crowd would have gathered round the pair at this stage urging the buyer to make a bid, however derisory.

'A charitable man might be inclined to make an offer but 'tis a cow I'm looking for, not a bicycle on four legs.'

At that the buyer would attempt to leave but the crowd would insist that he remain to receive the barbed line which was his due.

'I thought it was the blind pension you were looking for all right; will one of ye show him where the post office is when it opens.'

That would end the first round, and several such opening scenes would be enacted simultaneously around the fair field. I wondered how Squire Wallace would react to such insults or if the fair was beneath him.

The needs of the sellers were more urgent than those of the buyers who could dice with choice. Sellers might need the money to go towards a fortune to marry off a sister or a daughter into a farm with a good way of living or to help a member of the family to emigrate. The merchants also had to be paid before going on the book again until the next fair.

Far less ceremony and drama attended the women's dealings, giving the impression that they knew exactly what they wanted from the start. Buyers and sellers knew each other of old so that ducks, geese, turkeys, roosters, eggs, butter and feathers changed ownership within the hour. The stock were then left to squawk and babble while their owners went off to the waiting pubs. There they warmed to merriment and song with the help of hot punch and ham sandwiches. Out in the street the men got on with their ritual.

Our two female pigs changed into cash with a minimum of fuss before we reached Benmore, spotted by neighbouring farmers from Hare Mountain looking for patterns of sows.

The fair day coincided with Stepper's heat season. After exchanging our two patterns of sows we untackled her, removed her harness and left it in the cart. She seemed to know where we were going as we went round to McCarthy's yard where a sleek and frisky Irish draught stallion called Red Baron was at stud. As she approached the yard Stepper's excitement heightened but it was meekness itself compared with the neighing, bucking and racket of the stallion. Brad led Stepper into a high-railed corral outside the stables.

Ned Mack released the prancing, wild specimen with curved neck and flaring nostrils. Brad steadied Stepper as the Baron mounted, driving his rod into her after Con had adjusted its position. His powerful surges brought sparks from the cobble stones as iron shoes flashed with flint. Foam on surging flanks seemed to be a signal for Con to halt proceedings. Brad drew Stepper away while Con pulled back on a reluctant Baron causing that rod of multi-coloured muscle to plop from Stepper and squirt a few shots of cloudy liquid on to the cobblestones.

Excitement buzzed around our cart back on the street. We learned that Snake Mohan had planted a salmon but by the time he returned to the scene with the Sergeant the fish had been removed from our cart and replaced in Mohan's by a neighbour, Lily the Linnet, who saw through his plan.

'Keep away from him in future. There's a jealous badness in him towards us.'

'So you won't be doing any ploughing or spraying or mowing for him so?'

'Not if his was the last garden or meadow in the parish.'

'Great! Mother can't stand him either.'

'That's another thing: yourself and your mother, the way ye go about things.'

'The way we have to go about things; you can't do everything yourself.'

'Even if I could I wouldn't have sprayed for Squire Wallace.'

'He pays very good money, and you do other things for him – for the hunt.'

'That's a different traditional arrangement; the spraying machine is my own. I'm entitled to make my own protest.'

'About what?'

'About what? Well may you ask. There's blood on their money, the blood of my brother and my father and my sister; your own father's blood.'

Was my father's memory buried under continuous activity? Would this fit in with the compulsive neatness about everything Squire Wallace did? Could this man ask me to visit the manor, after killing my father before I was born? I wondered.

'So you won't be going back there again?' Brad probed.

'I have to go back the evening the next frost is due for the third spraying; I promised.'

'That'll burn off the stalks; are you sure that's what he wants?'

'That's exactly what he wants, and if you could till and spray and mow for people who take you for granted I think I can keep my promise to the squire. Anyway I have to study him to figure out a weakness, a way to get at him. We'll see about next year after this one is done.'

EIGHT

The drawing-room is what the squire called the oak-dominated spread to where his pull on a rope summoned Betsy. While he waited I noticed from papers on his desk that he was a baronet, addressed as Sir William Henry Wallace, Bart.

Betsy eyed me with dismay before being dispatched with an order for tea and sandwiches. Squire's tall majesty looked very much at home in these surroundings; the room could have been designed around him. But there was an agitation scratching inside him.

He probed my feelings towards my father. Out in the fields he had looked straight at me with every word and waited for my reply or observation. In this oak-walled sprawl he opened drawers as if he was searching for something and shut them again afraid of finding it. Betsy's timid entrance with a generous tray went unnoticed as once again she tried to comprehend my presence there. Curtsying to him with her tongue out, her departure brought him back to me. He nibbled; I devoured.

'You realise you were wrong, don't you, about killing my father? That's what's bothering you, isn't it?'

'I was wondering when – how this hour would come.'

I followed his eyes to those large well-kept hands now dragging his shoulders into a stoop.

Again the searching, now with a purpose. A wall panel flipped down revealing a drawer. A key rushed through its opening and a taped folder lay between us on the table.

Fingers tore open a pocket knife to gut the container of blood. Eyes burned their pleading into mine. Sandwiches moved outside our focus.

A piece of paper trembled from the envelope. Synchronised trembling of hands and voice.

'It was him or me: he was out of his mind with drink.'

I glared at his insult to my father.

'See these letters?' he indicated the manuscripts tied in string. 'These are his letters, your father's debate for these people against me and my kind, against my inherited rights in this barony. His native law and my planters' law not made for this place, clumsy law that could not match his adroitness.'

'Why have three of my family lost their lives here?'

'Why? Have you any idea of the several ways that word has gnawed its way under my skin since that night? A word that doesn't know night from day? Why? Why?'

'Did you hate my father?'

'No! I hated what he stood for and the inevitability of it. But not in my time: no; there are reasons for those rights. He wouldn't agree of course, but I still admired him. I had advised him to go away from here, see a bit of the real world and then come back to improve things for everyone.'

'And walk away from his MacRua duties so that you could keep your boot on Brad's neck?'

The wolfhound stirred.

'It's not like that. If I want anything killed it's this vendetta.'

'Murdered! My Dad was murdered! My Grandad and Aunt Ellen murdered, for what?'

The pitch of my voice brought the wolfhound to a stand. A stooped creature shuffled through another door enquiring if everything was in order and regarded me with a look he would give something dropped from the dog's rear end.

'Thank you, Andrew, and kindly ensure that we are not disturbed any further.'

He moved into the bay of the window, hands behind his back trying to squeeze a steadiness into his bother. 'I had arranged a good job for him with my cousin's estate in Essex so that he could experience our ways and try to understand us. He'd have done well there. Your father had class but he needed experience of the world outside of here.'

I tried to fit what I was hearing into everything I had heard. I blinked and renewed my glare: he looked away, and continued. 'I remain convinced he would have come back to lead this backward-looking place out of its peasant culture into the real world. A word from your father carried more power here than a column of cavalry.'

'Did he know about this?'

'He would go, he said, after he had done his duty here.'

Victoria barged through the guardian of her father's instructions. Her dark shoulder-length hair and beautiful cream floral dress could not hide an ugliness of attitude that was part of this spoilt brat, probably a year or two older than me. Her disdain matched my scorn.

'My goodness, Ranger, you don't mind who you mix with now, do you?' she mock-rebuked the wolfhound as she led him from the room.

'Yes; I always heard a dog will sniff along with any kind of a bitch?' I threw after her.

'Daddy! Did you hear what that – peasant said to me?'

'Yes, young man; I think that was uncalled for. My daughter's not accustomed to being addressed in that manner.'

'Your laws and our laws again, isn't it, Squire Wallace? Dish out the abuse, the killing, but can't take any back?'

Squire obviously was not accustomed to being addressed in that manner either. Victoria clung to the doorway, eyes and mouth open, budding breasts heaving on her chest.

'Kindly leave us, Victoria; we are in the course of a very difficult discussion.'

'Well!' The door crashed to her departure.

'You are a very spirited young man, speaking to me and my daughter like that; or is that your way of addressing everybody?'

'You know it isn't from the way we spoke before – this.'

'What age are you?'

'Sixteen, going on seventeen.'

'Sixteen, going on seventeen! Seventeen years I've carried this, damn you?'

He squeezed his anger in his fists. 'Why can't people accept how things have changed, improved?'

'There must have been a lot of room for improvement.'

We looked at each other. He looked away. 'I believe you are following the family tradition by taking fish from my rivers and game from my reserves?'

I had thought it was only the fish and game he was claiming. Now he seemed to think he owned the rivers and reserves as well. I would have to check this out.

'You're trying to water down your guilt for killing them, is that it?'

'I didn't kill them; not your grandfather or Miss Ellen. I was very fond of her: meant more to me than my mother.'

He gazed for a long time towards Benmore village. 'Will it ever end?' he whispered. He turned to me. 'I want you to accept these, your father's documents. Please try to understand and maybe even forgive me and my family.' He pushed a wooden box at me.

I took my father with me, leaving Squire standing there in the bay of the window.

He refused to rest in my hiding place in the loft. My sixteenth birthday had passed. His impatience with my secrecy jumbled my nightmares of his killing with my visions of him delivering speeches based on his manuscripts.

He chose the dark depths of a stormy Friday night to come to me. Laurie was out on his test night with Brad. Behind him on the wall the manor stables: he is outside, belligerent. Squire approaches with a man I do not know. Then it's him and Squire: he offers Squire a drink. Squire takes the bottle. He hands a package of documents to the squire, invites him to find a flaw in them. His father and Miss Ellen: shouting – Squire and my father, their faces close together. From behind the other man steals up: I shout but Dad doesn't hear. The man hits him over the head with a riding crop: Dad turns, hits him in the chest and watches him fall. Squire hits Dad over the head with the bottle and watches him crumble. He leaves the bottle beside him and helps the man away from the scene.

My eyes opened to the clatter of his box on to the floor, to see him fade into where the box had been. The storm stilled to witness my terror but raged again to urge me to the box. I lit the candle. The unlocked box would not open. I placed it on the bed and tried again.

'What is it, Cormac? What are you trying to do?'

Mother had stolen through my preoccupation and knelt beside me. The box opened to her touch, releasing the wild summer scent of Heather Hill.

Below in the kitchen the door scraped open and the storm rested. The candlelight picked out the tears on Mother's smiling face as she rocked to and fro cradling Dad in his box on her lap.

Laurie's face wore his 'never-again' look as he threw himself at his place in the bed. Brad quickly recognised the intruder in his wife's lap. I confirmed his suspicions and climbed down after him to the kitchen.

'Only my father and myself and the priest saw him after they killed him. She never saw him after he was boxed.'

'She'll be a while up there so?'

'She'll need a while. What's in the box? From the squire, I suppose?'

'Letters he had written about those rights; drawings and a photograph, and a few odd bits and pieces.'

'I remember. I'll go and sit with her; you'd better get into our bed.'

'Was your outing tonight as bad as it looks?'

'We'll have to talk, you and me, after this thing settles.'

It was an uneasy spring. Mother took the box as her own. While she fitted her jobs in their correct order between morning and night there were two worlds in the house: her world around Dad's box, and our world around silent prayers for normality. Brad waited and worked and waited. There were no messages. He ploughed and sowed. I kept the accounts and collected the money. I also attended secondary school whenever possible to prepare for matriculation examinations. Brad regarded that as downright selfishness, now that I had a good intermediate certificate. Recent events assured me that it was downright essential. I was now seventeen and knew that I would soon have to go out into the world that my father had not lived to see.

Uncle Danny's wedding day came that Shrove. They went. I stayed home to mind Laurie, Niamh and Mary. I had to think, to ponder on Brad's thinking and on how my father had taken possession of my mother.

'Please, Cormac, why don't you find Mammy's lonesome box and burn it?' Laurie pleaded.

'But it's not just her box; it's mine too, and Brad's.'

'Oh no it's not; she swore she'd kill anyone that touched it.'

'So you want her to kill me after I burn it?'

'She couldn't kill you; you're too strong.'

'And why's Mammy so cross all the time, Cormac? I can't ask her anything 'cause she won't hear me,' Niamh said.

'And Dad's as grumpy as a pig in nettles,' Laurie told the ground as if some action of mine could improve that situation. Children tugging at their pall of distress, on a spring day trying to be beautiful.

A bark and a scream from the byre split the tension. It was Mary again; Mary with her knack of being in the wrong place at the right time. She triumphantly held up something dark to glisten in the sunlight, while Polka tugged at her pinafore. Polka was having her first litter of pups, a distracting excitement poking a gap in the gloom of my thoughts.

Thoughts clawed through scattered happiness searching for reasons, causes. Questions stumbled over each other, leaving no space for answers as Laurie helped me with the milking. Questions longing for simple answers.

Niamh cuddling and running her fingers through weary little Mary's hair, hair she would earlier have extracted. Niamh in bed now, droopy-eyed, wondering when Mammy and Dad would be home after I had told a second story, Mary's head now sleeping on her shoulder. Another plea from Laurie as we lay on our bed in the stiff darkness. ''Tis that box, Cormac; 'tis carrying Mammy away from us, the way she won't see or listen, rocking away there with it in her lap.'

I tried to explain what I understood. I told him about my father.

Questions. 'How could he be your father if he died before you were born?' Questions. 'Boys stupid enough to kiss girls deserve whatever happens to them.' Laurie was adamant on this point.

Challenge: ''Tis up to you, Cormac; he's your father.' Tears; sleep, for Laurie.

My father, Brad's half-twin; Mother's . . . ? first love? only real love? Me: Love child? Mistake? Shameful reminder? Embarrassing emotional sore? Not for Mother, surely? But for Brad?

He said it. Many have remarked on my evolving strains of likeness to my father. Is that supposed to make me happy or guilty or impose compelling duty? How am I to fight his fight?

Brad: pillar of my life now in tremor as my instincts ponder a horizon his brother craved and Brad feared. Selfishness for me to respond to the lure of that horizon? Brad doesn't understand. The eyes drawn to that search are inside my head, inside every part of me. Even here in the dark my eyes that see are closed but that horizon is in full view, winking, beckoning, promising, never sleeping. I milk a cow, a goat, and it comes into the bucket. I write in the ledger and it flickers in the lamplight. I run, I race up the Glens and it adjusts to my rhythm, ever lightening my step. My real eyes looking, ears alert. Then without warning, anywhere, field, church, school, the eyes inside my head latch on to wonder; the intersecting worlds of Squire Wallace and my father; two beautiful girls, Margaret Wally and Mags-the-well; the matriculation examinations; chopping off Squire's power at the boundaries of Highgrove; the way the girls move to the music of my fiddle. What was Squire really trying to say?

England: if it is really that bad why are so many of our people doing so well there? Why the exodus of labour for 'the beet' each winter? Why? My father's 'why' aggravating Squire Wallace. So many whys nagging in my pillow.

Downstairs the front door scraped its telltale arc on the flagstone and back again as it closed. The darkness danced before Mother's candle checking our beds in the loft, darting shadows to her stealing footsteps. Pretended sleep becomes real, later disturbed by raised voices from their bedroom beneath. Brad's voice harrowing around the kitchen, intermittent, accusing.

Door opening to Granny Rua's old bedroom; her old bed creaks in sympathy with her son's agitation. Silent days darken into nights of children's whispers. Another day, another week, and another. Laurie and Niamh hide their unwanted food for Polka: Mother and Brad in opposite bedrooms: Mary's fun no longer finding a laughing response: Brad's face telling of pain, his words saying nothing, meaning gloom. And all this because of my father? Because of me being his son?

I fitted study into slots meant for other activities, trying to win Brad back by work at home. Anger: Brad's accusing wrath as we tended the ridges in the garden. 'You take no notice of me either, do you; not a damn bit of notice of what I say?'

'You're not saying much these times. No one is.'

'Only too well do you know what I'm saying. School beyond what's needed, putting you rightly above yourself, and everyone else.'

'It's not really the schooling, Brad, is it?'

His hoe tore at the earth, weeds and thinnings falling, but no words. I continued, ''Tis the worsening way with things inside at home, isn't it; that's if you could call it a home these times.'

'Oh, so it isn't good enough for our professor, is it? I told you, didn't I; warned you? Too much education destroys nature and manners and respect for people.'

'So you're happy with the way things are; is that what you're saying?'

'I'm a mile from happy with the way you are, if that's what you're asking.'

'You know very well what I'm asking. If you're that happy with the way things are at home try talking to Mother like you used to, unless you're afraid.'

He froze, like Granny Rua in death. I had accused him of fear. I tried to put it in context. 'I didn't mean it like that.'

'You'd know all about fear, wouldn't you?' He spat the words; their meaning stung. 'Fear: is that what's stopping you from doing your job inside that manor?'

'What job?' Surely he couldn't mean what was in his eyes.

'They're still alive, aren't they? Didn't roast to death in a fire yet, did they?' Yes, that's what he meant.

I realised we were on diverging paths. Admitting it to myself was a shock I was afraid to share. His voice again: 'And who caused all the trouble? You, by going up to Highgrove in spite of me. Of course you knew better, didn't you? Supping with his lordship in the manor and falling for his dirty trick to throw your father between your mother and myself.'

'I'm sorry.'

'Sorry! A lot of good that is now! Sorry! After turning your mother into a stranger to me – and my children.'

He was staring at me, shaking. The harder he gripped the handle of the hoe the more he shook. Reproach hurting in his eyes.

I moved towards him. 'I didn't want it to be this way.'

'Leave me alone.'

I stand, I gape, his eyes blinking wildness. I carry myself away, wondering. Pondering. More nights.

In some ways he is right. It is my fault. If I hadn't . . . if I had . . . if . . . I must speak to Mother. I try. She stares and walks through my words.

Niamh's night, empty stomach retching, shivering in a hot body; pain clutching her legs to her tummy. Guilt and fear: shame for causing the family turmoil which may have given rise to this. Fear, please God, don't let her die. Through Mother's door I carry her, protesting. Mother bewildered, then springing to Niamh's need.

'The doctor, Brad, Cormac, quick,' as she took Niamh to her.

'Better take the bike, Cormac,' from Brad in the doorway behind me.

Dr Fleming so fast: appendicitis; a race to the county hospital, wired message from doctor to surgeon while Mother and Niamh travelled in Crowley's hackney car. Next day, nothing. From the post office I phone the hospital. 'Operation just in time; Mother forgot to bring money to get home'. She's talking on the telephone, talking, giving instructions.

I find and hide my father's box before she gets home. Nothing about the box, everything about Niamh's narrow escape: her awful thirst after the operation, the hospital and all the people there who knew the family. Praise for Doctor Fleming's call to the hospital that ensured they were ready to operate on Niamh immediately on arrival.

Talk: everyone talking the old silence out of the house. Things to be done. Orders: had I any eyes in my head? Look at the state the house was in and she away for only a couple of days!

NINE

The world is thinking.

As Japan heals itself around the cancerous legacy of wartime misuse of atomic energy, the world powers sign treaties for its peaceful use. Electricity has found its way through the Glens along lines of black poles which are at odds with their surroundings. Brad is not impressed.

'Well, they're delighted with the electricity in Heather Hill since they got it. Danny can work later in the forge when they're busy.'

'That's right; rise up against me again.'

'It's not rising up! You have your views and I have mine. In this case I know mine are better.'

'Yours are better! God help you, boy. Don't you know what people are saying about you? Gallivanting to school when you should be out working like other lads your age! Nothing but harm in books beyond their time, poisoning your nature, softening the edge of what God gave you.'

The more Brad tried this line, the further I moved from his thinking. A reasonable matriculation certificate would make a bit of elbow room for my options beyond the Glens. Now that my father was properly laid to rest at home the battle of his life was still to be fought, his questions to be explored for answers.

Mutterings of grudging acceptance of Squire's unreasonable rights in the Glens and Hare Mountain still tangled in a maze of indecision. A barony, waiting. The rights assumed by Squire Wallace and his predecessors could be challenged only on the basis of their foundations, whether Brad liked it or not. But the only foundations Brad wanted dug were graves. While he saw merit in his brother's objectives he felt they were empty without first settling the score.

Settling the score? For whom? For what? To pour more blood into the Owmore? If this was a war between the Wallaces of Highgrove Manor and the MacRuas of the Glens, surely it was time we looked to our strengths; adopted a new strategy; chose when, where, and how the next battle would be engaged. Make the next battle the last one. Instead I felt like the last horse in the cavalry, having to figure out a strategy contrary to the goadings of Brad, my blinkered rider.

For me it was the week of the matriculation examinations. For Brad it was the excitement of a first week of exceptional crops of hay lying after his mowing machine. Afterwards the awkward little hill meadows awaited my scythe, this time lightened by the curious company of Laurie, Niamh, baby Mary, Loopy and Polka, after examinations and on Saturdays.

But that time was not summer for Mother. Each morning saw her leaving the milking and retching to emptiness at the end of the byre. Brad had always left for someone else's meadow. She was happy that he had at last mastered the commercial reality of trading services for cash. The arms of my seven hill customers were still too short to reach through tradition to the bottoms of their pockets, all except Jamey Casey whom I was surprised had any money at all. A day in his hilly meadow was worth a shilling, and no patronising instructions.

'There's something addling you, isn't there, young Cormac?' Mother observed in the byre as we milked adjacent cows in rhythm.

'Look who's talking, and your stomach heaving your guts these past weeks.'

'Ah, the worst is over; another week should do it. Don't be dodging my question.'

'I'm sick of it, these excuses of men watching me mowing their hilly old meadows and blathering on about old Brad and my father and your Brad.'

'Comparing you to them, you mean?'

'Maybe 'tis all right to be compared, interesting sometimes; but not by loafers who can't work to warm themselves.'

She was laughing; a motherly laugh scattering light through my gloom. 'I wouldn't trust you but you'd say it to them too?'

'Three more days will finish them. Brad won't like it but I'm done with slavery after that. And yes, of course I'm going to tell them what I think.'

'Don't be too sure about Brad not liking it; don't be so sure at all.'

The sun could have cleared the sky to have a really good look at them that June Sunday morning after first Mass. Light floral dresses teased my eye with the allure of Mags-the-well and Margaret Wally as they licked something white and creamy outside Markey's shop. 'Like a pair of kittens in a dairy ye are; what's that ye're savouring?'

'Ice-cream, Cormac. Have a bit of mine,' Margaret said.

'And mine's a choc-ice out of the new fridge,' Mags interjected. 'You must try a bit of mine too.'

My bite on Margaret's sent ice-cream bulging out of its wafers. Her tongue and lips took sultry control of the sumptuous mess as something in her eye hinted fun.

Mags treated her choc-ice to a cross between kissing and

licking. It was held on a stick, so I nibbled rather than bit my sample. In both instances the initial chilly shock left an aftertaste which had me marvelling at the possibilities of application of electricity. Lights, plugs delivering power to boil a kettle, chill an ice-cream, weld a gate and bringing more power to radio than many would have wished.

And two girls' lips and tongues on cool ice-cream, mischievous eyes arousing thoughts I should not be thinking after Mass on a June Sunday.

'My Dad wants you to spray our garden this week if you can,' Margaret said.

'And Mother wants you to do ours as well,' Mags added, with a nudge to Margaret.

'I'll teach you how to use a knapsack,' I teased back. Mags' garden wasn't much bigger than a kitchen floor. Her only sister Peggy, a bulky black-haired image of her mother, was a knitter who could never seem to produce enough sweaters for her first cousin's shop in Chicago, even with the help of Mags and her mother. Even our nearest neighbour Nancy Boyle, after her elderly husband Brendan had suffered a stroke that only half-killed him, had taken to knitting Peggy's designs to a target of two a week.

'I'll be crossing Owmore River to the Manor on Monday so I'll fit your gardens in after that.'

The only trace of the ice-cream and choc-ice were faint moustache effects on their upper lips as they nudged and pulled each other with giggling whispers.

'You said you'd ask him,' from Mags.

'But 'twas you showed it to me. You ask him.'

Margaret blushed.

'Maybe if you could come late, Cormac,' Mags suggested.

'Yes; couldn't you leave our garden till last?'

They were saying more than they were speaking. The eyes, the nudges, the childhood mischief spiced with an earthy excitement hummed through those floral dresses.

'I was thinking we might check out the woods for that fox after the supper?' Brad suggested during the milking that evening in the byre. Assuming that it was me and not Mother he addressed I agreed, adding that a few hours in the woods were overdue on my part.

Later, as we allowed Loopy and Polka to do their own exploration, I realised the fox that had left our yard as hungry as it had come during the past week was a suggestion for Mother's ears only.

'What are we going to do about Laurie?' He left his question hanging in the sunset between us as he surveyed a fallen beech. Laurie's trips into the woods had failed to get him on Brad's wavelength with nature.

'But he's only eight or nine years old; he might change yet.'

'At his age you and your father and myself and all before us could name and shape every sound in this forest.'

'Well, he's not interested yet anyway. If anything he's pulling against it; so maybe you should wait until something stirs him.'

'So you think there might be some flicker?'

'The way I see it is this: Niamh is very well up on the sounds and she has a nose for the scents as well. He might have to learn fast to answer her questions after I'm gone.'

'After you're gone where?'

'Depending on the examination results, probably England.'

'England! More dreaming like your father! Damn it, Cormac, you're at a stage when you can do everything around here and now you're off to the land of the heathen, leaving me stuck here with no help. You can't go yet I'm afraid, my boyo; not yet, not for a long time yet.'

I knew Brad well enough not to argue with an eruption like that while it was still hot. I moved after him to a point where the forest made a steep descent to Owmore River. Even in the dusk of a Sunday evening, and with other matters on his mind, he moved with the wary poise of a poacher.

'Why should it have to happen to me? Is there some kind of a *mí-ádh* on me or what?'

'Does it have to be the eldest son? Maybe one of the others . . .'

'I'm the tenth eldest-son in the line. Now my eldest son might as well be a girl for all the concentration or interest he has in the wild.'

I allowed him to settle as the twilight sharpened the sounds and scents all around us. His mood was in sad contrast to his excitement of only a few years ago as he fed my hunger for the ways of the wild. He spoke again. 'You could have a point there; I could be depending on you yet.'

His statement sent my mind into a spin. Depending on me for what? To train Laurie as Brad had trained me? To train Niamh or Mary or . . . ? Surely not to assume the mantle of Brad after him? No, surely not. Anyway that was too far in the future to consider. Perhaps he sensed my confusion just as I sensed that he had more on his mind.

'I believe you've decided to spray for the squire again?'

'Yes; I'm starting in the morning.'

'That'll look really bonny all right; the son of Cormac MacRua at Squire Wallace's service.'

'That's not the way I see it.'

'Suffering Christ, boy, haven't you any pride? Is the money that important that you'd betray your own father?'

'Believe me, Brad, I have pride. You think the squire is using me! Fine: I hope he thinks so too, but I'm thinking ahead; five years; more, maybe less; something I picked up at school, or somewhere. Meantime while I'm around here I'll provide a service and get paid for it. There's dignity in that, depending on how it's done, and pride. I don't have to hide inside small-mindedness, especially when I'll be expecting, *demanding* big-mindedness from the squire when my father's time comes.'

He searched my eyes in a way he hadn't done before. 'I hope you know what you're doing, because I don't.'

'To be honest I'm not that sure yet myself, except about one thing.'

'Yes: abandoning your place as fast as you can.'

'No; yes; going away for a reason. No, the one thing I'm certain of is this: you've said it, the master said it and my father was sure of it. If I'm to get anywhere in my dealings with the squire it'll have to be as an equal, at his level.'

For a moment he said nothing but his body reaction signalled what was coming. 'Dangerous ideas just like him — and silly! God help us, boy; you equal with the squire! At one level with him!'

The same old perspective: to Brad, levelling meant bringing Squire down. I let it pass.

'Ah well, 'twon't be long more before life will hang an anchor on your madness. Coming out of the Glens and one level with the squire!'

He walked back the way we had come. He hadn't mentioned the vendetta, the blood. I waited, before rejoining him.

'I'll see if I can get Laurie interested; that's if you'd like . . . '

'Oh go ahead, go ahead. You'd better pray for a miracle as you're at it or send him to Knock, like Granma Healy.'

My promise to Brad took precedence over the one to Mags

and Margaret, so it was the second round spraying near the end of July when they arranged to meet me after I finished the gardens in their area. More giggling but the dusk gave Margaret the courage to blurt their purpose. 'Slow kissing, Cormac, did you ever do it?'

Her question didn't seem to make sense. Slow kissing! Just how long could you dawdle over a kiss? Certainly no longer than a few seconds.

'Well, Cormac, did you?' Mags prompted.

'No; you're up to your tricks again, the pair of you?'

'Honest, Cormac; 'tis in a magazine from Mags' cousin in Chicago; well, 'twas sent to her sister with photos of people wearing some of the jumpers she knitted. Mags found the bit about the slow kissing on the back of a pattern page. She showed it to me; honest.'

'So have you tried it out yourselves?'

Brief giggles and nudges before Mags took her turn. 'That's why we wanted to meet you at night, Cormac. You're the only one we could ask.'

'The only one we could trust,' Margaret affirmed.

'And we can't delay long; you know the questions that would be asked.'

'And I'll be up half the night to finish a jumper with a new stitch she's after designing,' Mags complained.

'So what am I supposed to do; was there any attempt at a description of this kissing?'

'You won't tell anyone, sure you won't, Cormac?' Margaret pleaded.

'And we won't tell a living soul either,' Mags added, to seal the bargain.

They had agreed that Margaret would go first and that Mags would give directions. Margaret turned her face to me and placed her hands on my shoulders. Like the curtain opening at the parish concert, the clouds allowed a gap for the moon to have a peep. Her face was lovely – no, beautiful, eyes closed, black hair falling down her back.

'Go on, Cormac.' The first instruction from Mags stirred my anxiety.

'God, I'm not washed or anything. I'm all sweat and bluestone, and I should have shaved.'

'You're grand; you'll do fine the way you are,' Mags urged.

Margaret opened her eyes and raised herself on the balls of her feet to signal her agreement.

Her lips puckered into the shape of a kiss. I inclined my mouth towards hers but had to figure out what to do with my nose. I decided to go left and placed my slowest effort on those lips that must now have that crampy feeling, like holding a smile too long for a camera.

'I think you're supposed to wait for me, Cormac.'

'Yes, Cormac; you're supposed to wait for Margaret.'

Not wanting to spoil everything I tried again. I kissed and waited, and waited. I brought my nose round to the other side and kissed again. She softened her lips, and kissed me back.

'I think you're supposed to have your arms around her, Cormac,' the instructor observed, just as the thought had tempted myself.

I ventured about the middle of her back with one hand. Margaret moved one of hers round the back of my shoulder. I tried my right hand between her shoulder blades; hers came around my other shoulder.

'Around his neck I'd say, Margaret.'

Margaret did as she was told but added a move of her own by bringing her body against mine. Through my shirt the thrill of her contact, breasts to my hammering chest, lips moving with mine like the way she teased that ice-cream. The tip of her tongue searched my lips, strange wild feelings, wanting skin to tingling skin.

'It seems to be the devil's own magic! Lovely I'd say!' Mags interrupted.

I looked to the moonlit clouds. Margaret gripped my shirt, her forehead against my chest. 'Yes, Mags; it is lovely, really lovely.'

'I'd better have my turn so, Margaret; 'tis getting late, and you know . . . '

'I know; the sister's jumper.'

'You'll tell us what to do so, won't you?' They exchanged places.

Though she was about the same height as Margaret, there was more of Mags to fill my arms. A buxom feel, a different scent. Again the ready lips, the upturned face, wild chestnut hair. It was easier for me to start this time. Loose kisses on those lips like Mags did to that choc-ice. But the choc-ice didn't kiss back like this, a strong, almost sucking movement.

'You should close your eyes, Cormac,' Margaret offered.

'How am I doing, Margaret?' Mags wondered.

'Relax a bit I'd say, Mags; you're very stiff looking.'

An apologetic little shrug from Mags looking up at me. I drew her to me and caressed the back of her neck. She felt different, almost like a baby or a cat responding to my hands. She began to purr, a soft little moan leaving her lips there for me, reacting by adjusting the position of her face. Choc-ice teasing of lips: tasting each other, wanting more. Feelings too good to be wrong thrilled in a rising chase.

'Well, what do you think of it, Mags?'

No reaction from Mags. A fistful of chestnut hair won the attention Margaret wanted. Kissing interrupted, Mags also rested her head against my chest. 'True for you, Margaret; lovely altogether. Makes you feel all funny inside, doesn't it?'

125

'And makes you forget about the jumper you were in such a fuss about.'

'Oh, blast that sister and her new designs.'

'Good night, girls; I have to go.' Something strange was about to happen if I stayed, something I couldn't control.

'Ah, Cormac,' from both of them.

My shortcut from Hare Mountain to the Glens took me across the Owmore river at the sally ford. As I splashed through the ford there was a balm about the water. I threw my boots, trousers and shirt on the Glens bank and swam upstream. The feeling was good, easing the confused thrills lingering from the girls. Two torchlights picked me out from the Hare Mountain bank.

'Who are you? What do you think you're doing in there at this hour?' The uneasy reality of Brad's warnings.

'You must have nothing pulling at your mind when you're at the river.'

But I wasn't poaching. With my name I would have a job to convince them. Anger at the squire, at the system and laws that had guard and bailiff patrolling 'his' waters.

'I'm having a swim and a wash but if that's against the law, goodnight.'

I swam downstream and escaped into the night with a new understanding of my father's wishes.

Riding Squire's bay stallion with a saddle was another new thrill of that summer, and my handling of him drew haughty glances from Victoria. I had arranged a Saturday for the third spraying of his potato garden. It was a traditional country holiday weekend and the date of the second hunt at Highgrove Manor, starting at noon. The date also seemed to be Victoria's eighteenth birthday.

If I was to be honest, the extra care I was taking over the garden was a delaying tactic. Squire must have interpreted it at face value because he surprised me with another invitation to the manor when I had finished.

'There are things I need to discuss with you, young MacRua, arrangements to be made, possibly . . . ' That was how he addressed me as we munched sandwiches on the now very busy lawn.

'Got a new recruit for us then, Sir Henry?' from a lady bearing a strong resemblance to her jaunty speckled gelding.

'Hope you hadn't any major plans for the afternoon?' the squire posed the question to me.

'Plans? Yes, I suppose, but nothing major.'

'Perhaps you'd like to join us in the hunt? Pick any horse you like in the stables.'

I packed a sandwich into my mouth to allow me time to chew on the enormity of the invitation. The hunt was 'them', and we were – well, Brad and I had spotted two possible foxes they could chase today. We were ghillies; we were 'us'.

If I were to ride in this hunt what would that do to my relationship with Brad? What indeed would it do for my relationship with the squire?

Knowing the squire's methodical ways, this apparently casual invitation must have been well considered. Why? What was in it for him? Appeasement? Putting me in my place for my attitude to Victoria, that indulged bitch of an only child?

'Any horse I like?' I enquired as casually as I could.

'Good! I like a chap with a bit of . . . what do you call it? Spunk, yes. Carmody will fix you up with some gear while you're down there. Better hurry, though; we'll be riding out any moment.'

'You! In the hunt? And surely not on King Henry?' Victoria erupted as I prepared the bay stallion.

'Any horse I like includes King Henry, unless you consider your authority greater than your father's.'

The white face, the big eyes, the heaving bosom, the mouth opening and closing like a fish facing upstream. 'You – you – ignorant peasant! You – bastard.'

I spat at the superiority in her eyes. Spurs to pony's flanks, and she was gone, long stirrup, upright, perfect position.

Tiny Carmody swung from the base of the hayloft and dropped into the manger, a manoeuvre he had obviously perfected over the years. 'Christ, Cormac boy, you don't give a rotten spud about her, do you? Not one bit afraid of her or nothing?'

Tiny's tongue probed the gap where his front teeth used to be, blue eyes sparkling in admiration under eyebrows straining upwards.

'You're not afraid of her, are you, Tiny?'

A spit shot through the gap in his mouth. He removed his cap and clutched it to his chest, the wrinkles on his forehead rippling back to his poll. The blue eyes were serious, looking up into mine. 'The devil himself! I swear to God you can ask anyone in Highgrove and they'd rather lay eyes on the lad with the horns than on that virago. 'Tis a different place entirely when she's away at that college.'

The hunting horn sounded on the lawns. I cantered off after fourteen horses and twenty beagles heading towards the fens, the only part of the estate allowed to remain wild as a haven for game.

Brad would have given the fox three minutes. The hunt was on, the beagles yelping in excitement at the fresh scent. I held King Henry to observe the action. Though Victoria drove her pony hard with spurs and whip she gradually lost ground, finding it more difficult to negotiate the fences. She solved her problem during the regroup by claiming a hunter from a grovelling young man who assisted her into the saddle.

'A likely young man for Victoria's hand in marriage,' the comrade mount of the speckled gelding advised as we rode off for the kill.

Later in the evening I watched the fox playfully performing manoeuvres to confuse the pack, crossing his own trail, going to and fro through the same ditch or fence in different places and finally heading for the cover of the steep cliff to the Owmore river. Victoria saw what I was observing and spurred the hunter into the chase.

'You silly bitch,' I muttered as I drove King Henry after her, afraid she would spur the hunter to jump the fence.

A hundred foot drop into the river awaited them. The hunter swerved in mid-jump, falling sideways on to the fence and sending Victoria hurtling over it. The fox had escaped. Flashes: Aunt Ellen: the rest of the hunt on a criss-cross trail.

I abandoned King Henry. I wanted to see her dead – no, humbled, held somewhere in the bushes and rhododendrons. The hunter was caught in the ditch, but support for his neck gave him enough leverage to get upright. Victoria clung to an ancient blackthorn, parallel with the vertical cliff. She had a bird's-eye view of the river far below. 'Help me! Help me! Oh God, help me!'

In less than a minute she would drop to her death. I could wait or rejoin the hunt: nobody would notice. A long road that has no turning, an account to be settled, the books balanced. Debit Old Brad, Aunt Ellen, my father; credit the entire haughty offspring of Sir William Henry Wallace Bart.

'Help me, oh please!'

I know what Brad would do; what he would want me to do. Oh God, I can't let this happen.

'Count to ten; hold on tight. I'll get a grip on you.'

I swing through the rhododendron. Terror pleading in her face. I anchor myself, get a grip on her legs. She lets go.

'Easy now; work with me and I'll get you out.'

I grip her jodhpurs by the belt from the back. She groans as I put my head between her legs, shoulders at the front so that her crotch rests on the back of my neck.

'I'm going to lift and pull you now, so bite on your sleeve or something.'

Gradually I got her on to the fence. She was crying, tears gushing from frightened eyes. 'I never realised – look – thanks,' she sniffled. I pressed away the tears with my thumbs. Hysterical sobs, eyes like an injured fawn. If only I could kiss the pain from her pleading face. The beagles arrived followed by the rest of the hunt. I remounted King Henry and left her colleagues to fuss over her.

Tiny Carmody was delighted. Brad was not delighted. Mother's mind was divided. I knew my father would have understood. Definitely Dad would have understood; I could feel it.

'A hero!' Brad mocked.

'What would you have done?'

'They must all be dancing in heaven.'

'No one deserves to die like that.'

'God sends His vengeance and a MacRua interferes.'

He had a point. By those standards I had failed my family by not doing nothing. I heard him continuing. 'The one part of the cliff with a straight drop, the place my sister was thrown from.'

'Maybe they'd all prefer to rest in peace.'

He grabbed me by my shirt, popping the buttons. His mouth opened and closed, eyes flashing in a tight white face, before throwing me from him. 'And you call yourself a MacRua?' he said as I stood.

I chose not to tell Mother about the incident with Brad. There were more gardens in the last round of spraying to be completed: I would do these as promised, keep out of everybody's way until my examination results arrived and then leave to find my own life. If I wasn't worthy to be called a MacRua, if I could rescue the enemy from death, then I should leave the responsibilities of my inheritance to someone else. I should take my shame to where nobody but myself would be aware of it.

TEN

It was during that spraying that my education met another reality, starting with Moll Flood as she accompanied me to her garden, seated beside me on the spraying machine.

'And how's Tom Flood keeping?' I enquired about her husband, one of those at the rambling house whose curiosity about my pubic hairs I had thwarted.

'Ah, sure the back is at him again, stuck to the bed able to do nothing – nothing.'

'Oh, I'm sorry to hear that. How're you managing?'

Her eyes searched my question, interesting wide-set eyes enhancing a tanned face under an unruly crop of auburn hair tied in a ponytail. 'My brother comes down for the milking. Everything else is as good as can be, in the circumstances.'

We turned into her garden by the river. I jumped off. Her jumping crash-tackle brought me to the ground as I turned to help her down. She resumed her teasing as we loaded the next barrel.

There was a southerly turn in the breeze, and a sultry cloud drooped over Mahonys' Gap on Hare Mountain.

'You're like a setter pointing a pheasant. What's wrong?'

'The wind is turning. If it has blight on it and it gets in at the gap it'll have a free run through the valley.'

'I see. Is there anything I can do?'

'Could you get a message to Mahony's to be ready for me when I finish Bill Daly's?'

'So you can't come to the house for tea or anything, so?'

'There'll be plenty of time for eating after dark. I have to fight the blight till then.'

'Promise! Come on! Promise that you'll call back to me after you finish. I'll have something nice ready for you.'

That night, on the soft cool aftergrass beside her garden, Moll answered questions I had never thought of asking as I satisfied her craving for what old Tom Flood could not give.

Next day the examination results arrived. Better than expected, definitely a wide range of options for continuing education or for employment. Mother congratulated me. Brad continued to ignore me. As I quietly gathered a few basics to take with me to London, Betsy Foran brought me a letter from Victoria.

Highgrove Manor
Thursday

Dear Cormac MacRua

I owe you an apology, and would prefer to speak to you in person. Could you please meet me tonight at the bend of the avenue where the sycamores form an arch, say around 10.00. Mother is home in the Manor, hence this arrangement.

I will wait in anticipation.

V. W.

I fitted the books and clothes I needed into a half-sack and cycled with them to the railway station at Ballybo to book myself in for the first train in the morning. Then it was back to Benmore to say a long goodbye to Margaret Wally and on to my meeting with Victoria. I left my bike inside the gate and jogged along the avenue. She was leaning against a sycamore at the second bend dressed in tennis whites. I stopped. She approached me, her hand extended. I decided to take it.

'I'm very sorry for the horrible things I've said.'

'All right after your fright, are you?'

'Oh my God, how can I ever thank you!'

For some reason I remembered that I hadn't been to the river for a swim since my visit with Molly.

'I'm going away for a while.'

'Oh, I didn't know. What a shame. I – would you like to sit with me on the rug over there?'

I hesitated.

'For a little while, please.'

There was something plaintive in her 'Please'. She walked off: I followed her into the shrubbery. She knelt on the rug, and indicated for me to join her. I remained standing.

'You're so very strong, the way you lifted me and pulled us both back up.'

'That's just the way I am.'

'Can I ask you a big favour, please.'

I knelt on one knee opposite her.

'The way you wrapped me around your neck, the way you held me, could you do it again please?'

'Here?'

'Please.' That word again; the way she said it.

She stood and spread her legs. I inclined my head and she climbed into position, knees to the front, crotch on the back of my neck. Only this time it really was her crotch, bare under her white tennis skirt. Her hands went inside my waistband and pulled at my pants. I placed her back on the rug; she drew me to her. I hesitated; she clung on.

The impossibility of the situation and the enormity of the opportunity temporarily stunned me. Suddenly she was very beautiful, at least in a physical way. But there was anger in my passion as I ripped off her top and we tore at each other, before I drove my anger into her.

I related the story to Brad as if it were premeditated revenge. He rejoiced at the desolation I had caused, a MacRua screwing Squire's family in the most appropriate way possible.

There was a lighter shade on my shame as I rattled and rolled my way to London.

ELEVEN

London, opportunity city: offices; black-smoke chimneys, factories, building sites, services, police, transport, jobs everywhere. Not a sign of blue smoke anywhere. A different world, nothing like home. A million smells forming grime in the fumes: double-decker buses, each holding more people than Reillys' rambling house, trucks, cars, a bustle of people grinding out their activities, people of different colours, amazing accents, ignoring each other, puzzled by my salutations. Bigger, brighter and more exciting than I could have imagined by night; a different scene on the same stage; styles of dress foreign to Benmore or Ballybo.

Trains running underground. Yes; full trains travelling through tubes under the city, and following the expansion of the city into neighbouring counties. Jobs, vacancies everywhere. But some notices displayed their bleak preference: 'No Irish, No Blacks'. Landladies' handwritten signs hung starkly in their windows: 'No Irish No Dogs No Blacks'.

Where to fit in, to find a toehold in the tumult. Only twenty-five hours since stepping on to the Euston station platform, awed, excited. A sense of freedom where nobody expected me, where I knew nobody. Parks in the middle of the jostling streetscape, little oases of manicured nature. Benches, some becoming beds at night. In here an escape to my music, a gift from the master. 'It will travel the world with you and never let you down,' he had promised.

Noon September sun on my face, eyes closed, playing through

my new perceptions. 'Bonny Prince Charlie', 'Ye Banks and Braes', a few lilting jigs; applause, coins dropping into my fiddle case. A request: 'Play "It's a Long Way to Tipperary", young fellow.' Spirited old men limp through a march, heads erect shouldering imaginary guns. And the women had to have their request: 'Marie's Wedding'. A policeman on horseback checks out the hooley. The men mention places in Europe where comrades, who should be here, lie in foreign soil but are not forgotten. I am invited up to the Veterans' Home specially to play 'The Londonderry Air' for old Billy and Madge, and Matron. More coins, and lamb stew.

'So you're from over there,' Matron observes.

'Over where?'

'Ireland of course! Where do you think?'

'Yes; Kerry. And you?'

'Doesn't the accent say it all? Enniskillen, County Fermanagh. You over here long?'

'About twenty-eight hours.'

'Where are you stayin', or headin'?'

'Just looking around; nowhere to stay, yet. No great welcome for us Irish around here, is there?'

'Ignorance, that is; jumped up bitches, some of them landladies; a penny looking down on a ha'penny.' She lit a cigarette, and took a good look at me.

'There's a big attic up here being converted. You can kip down for a few nights while you're lookin' round.'

'If it's not too much trouble; I'll pay my way.'

'Are you any good at figures; accounts, headache stuff like that?'

'Yes: figures are fun when you get them working for you.'

'Right: I've a better idea, you can figure your way. Where's your luggage?'

'That's it; there's my fiddle and there's my sack.'

'A touch of Dick Whittington about you, is there? And what's in the sack?'

'A shirt, couple of pairs of socks, jumper, underwear and books.'

'Hope there's a lot more inside your head, my wee lad. 'Tisn't in sweet County Kerry you are now, you know. And what'll we be calling you?'

'Cormac – Cormac MacRua. And you?'

'Ethel Gibbons; back home a black Prod; over here as green as yourself. You've crafty eyes in a young head. What age are you at all?'

I hesitated. Her look softened, like a mother's. 'You can tell me. Then we'll decide what age you should be.'

'I'll be nineteen in January.'

'Will you look at the great adventurer, my eighteen-year-old.'

'Almost nineteen. I got myself over here didn't I, and I've made more money in a day than I thought I could make in a week.'

'Oh I'm sorry, I'm sure! You'll pass for twenty-one. That raw look when you get angry will carry it easily.'

A bath in a big enamel fixture under taps spouting hot and cold water. A toilet with a water system to flush away what one left in it. Bath and toilet sharing a small room all to themselves!

Three days became three weeks and into the new year past my birthday in the Veterans' Home.

Veterans' Home
London SW1
31/1/58

Dear Mother, Brad and family

Thanks for the birthday wishes and letter with all the news. I'm glad you're all keeping well. I intend getting home for a few weeks to help out in the summer.

Please don't keep worrying about me, Mother. To be honest there are days when I don't think of any of you, except at night if I remember to whisper a few prayers. There's a college near here called a polytechnic where they have all sorts of courses by day and in the evenings. You can mix your subjects to get a diploma, so I am studying agriculture and land surveying parttime, basic land law included. Method in my madness, I hope. I can understand your advice about getting a regular job but I'm making a lot more money and enjoying my variety of options the way things are. When I explore the rivers and waterways I bring back fish and get well paid for them.

I have a few regular spots where I play the fiddle and the money I get is better than for spraying.

They don't have fairs like ours here, but the markets are along the same lines. Ethel Gibbons gives me a bonus on what I save when I haggle for the supplies for the Home every week. Like our fairs, it's all over very fast and very early in the mornings. So in a way I am working regularly, and studying a bit. No two days are the same.

Thanks for giving me Betsy Foran's address where she's training for nursing. It's a long way from here but I'll try to get to see her. To prove that it's money season here I enclose a £20 note.

You were probably right not to give my address to Squire Wallace. I don't know what he would need it for anyway. But it's all right to give my address to Margaret Wally.
I must go now. I love you all.
Yours always
Cormac

Of course I had a good idea as to why the squire needed my address and so did Brad.

The March day in 1958 that Nikita Khrushchev took over as premier of the USSR from Nikolai Bulganin was more memorable in my world as the day I met student nurse Betsy Foran in Epping. As a preliminary to entering training for general nursing, she was one of a group of ten Irish girls studying children's nursing. She was different, thinner and more attractive in the uniform. Thinner because she was hungrier.

The casual amount of cash in my pocket financed a feast, a sort of barbecue in nearby Epping Forest.

Stories from home, music on the fiddle, singing, dancing and my stories from the city. Envy at the freedom of my unusual lifestyle.

Epping Forest could have breakfasted on our forest back in the Kerry Glens and hardly noticed. Betsy and I found ourselves walking to a vantage point from where she showed me a bigger version of Highgrove Manor owned by cousins of Squire Wallace and where Betsy escaped every fourth weekend for a working break. So this was where the squire had arranged that my father could have based himself to explore the world beyond the Glens.

General Phillips constantly complained of how difficult it was to acquire and keep reliable help, Betsy assured me, so there would be suitable work on the estate if I wanted it. She became flustered in trying to retrieve her words, apologising that I had my sights set at another level.

I held her. We kissed in that slow way I had learned with Margaret and Mags. She responded, clinging, sighing, hoping we could meet again, just ourselves without the pressure of a nurses' home curfew and curiosity of student mates. Her kiss, the way she felt, lingered on my way back to London on the train as day became night, reviving memories of that wild night with Moll Flood when she drove me to a frenzy, and then later more slowly to another in the field behind her house. A night of new ecstasy and lingering questions.

Pity for Moll as she craved for love and fun and excitement in a marriage to a man who could grapple to examine the pubic hairs of fifteen-year-old boys in the rambling house but failed in the real test of intimacy.

Back at the Veterans' Home letters await from Margaret Wally, Mags-the-well and the master. The Leaving Certificate examinations are Margaret's immediate horizon but I am dreamed into her feelings. She asks me to tell her about mine but to be careful what I might say as her mother might read the letter, asking for a photograph in return for her own enclosed and sure we would meet when I got home in the summer.

Mags had finished with school and was turning out four jumpers a week. Not a lot of contact with Margaret Wally because she was busy studying. Loads of news, and guess what, a blooming miracle: Moll Flood was expecting a baby and Tom, her creaking old husband, did an about-turn at death's door. Mags couldn't wait for a bit of gas during my holidays.

Moll expecting! Am I involved? Was that how she schemed her plans? And if I am involved there, what about Victoria? Consternation should be bulging the manor walls by now. The poacher's revenge: how would they feel about it, my father, his father, Aunt Ellen? Especially Aunt Ellen in this reversal of roles?

The master was glad I was keeping up the music and wished he could be young again where I now found myself. I shouldn't worry about Mother's concern that I should find a steady job; that was only natural for mothers.

I was young and educated and blessed with uncanny native instincts. I should establish no ties, just follow the spirit, the dreams in my heart in the short time available before some lassie would put an anchor on me as her husband. No point in regrets then. And be sure to call, for a few drinks and to swap a few tunes during the holidays.

From college library to land registry the lecturers showed me how to trace the Phillips Estate, twelve hundred acres of Essex with extensive fishing and gaming rights extending into Epping Forest East. I would have to get inside the workings of this place, this extension to his education the squire had agreed with my father.

Colonel Thompson, the general's agent, was surprised but pleased with my proposal to act as occasional ghillie for hunting and fishing trips and noted that I could actually be contacted in my London base by telephone. A guide and horse were provided to allow me to explore the layout of the estate and its extended rights. Unlike Highgrove, however, these rights were owned by the smallholders and leased back to the Estate.

It took two long weekends and my first painful encounter with a pike to complete the initial survey. There was an abundance of game. The waters carried coarse fish such as perch, pike and eels, but not many trout or salmon, as I discovered the night an eighteen-pound pike gripped my fingers for bait as my hand dangled among the reeds in the river.

Disappointment from the colonel that I would be on holidays for the first hunt, particularly for the visit of the General's Wallace cousins from Ireland. I wondered if they were aware of Victoria's condition but I couldn't ask. How was I supposed to know?

First holidays. Air buoyant with the scented freshness of Mother's shrubs and herbs, blue smoke in a blue sky, suggesting the warm aroma of peat. Shy first reception from Laurie, Niamh and Mary; the twins pulling at me and exploring my bags. Later a long hug from Mother and tears of joy. Everybody looking great except Brad; tired, trying to cope with too much on his own.

Laurie now eleven, not very fond of farmwork, wanting to be at stonework with his Uncle Peter. I bring him with me on the spraying machine, show him how to handle different horses, how to reassure them with the soft cadence of Irish poetry in their ears. He loves the machine, is curious about its workings, packing the drive chamber, pressure through the vacuum chamber. Still no interest in fishing or hunting, unlike nine-year-old Niamh. Brad cannot accept this. The knowledge cannot be handed on to a girl.

Rhetorical questions from Laurie: 'Who taught the stag to pick up a scent on the breeze? Who taught Loopy and Polka to pick out whistle calls at impossible distances?' Questions he daren't ask Brad: 'What was so special about catching salmon anyway? Or culling deer? Surely it was cruel to take a wild kid goat and kill it and eat it, even if it is rejected by its mother?'

Where Laurie was concerned the poacher ethos was just a game, a vanity he hated and didn't want to understand.

Questions about England from Mother, from the children. Mary wants to know how the people of different colours make themselves that way or if God uses boot polish on them before giving them to the nurses.

Brad waits until we are on our own in the fields. 'It didn't happen.' Disappointment in his voice.

'I was talking to him. He'll never take to it now.'

'Not that: not Laurie; Squire's daughter, she didn't take.'

'Oh?'

We stood there among our thoughts, looking towards the manor. Words could not relate the hope to which he clung in his disillusionment. My feelings swarmed around the contradictions in that hope. We spoke of normal things on our way to see the master.

'Tis hard going without you, very hard.'

'Do you really have to do all that work?'

'Sure no one else has any machinery.'

'Can't you hire someone?' It was good to join the lilt of conversation with him.

'And have them break all round them! No; 'tis myself the people want to see coming.'

'Brad; honest to God, you're getting very old looking.'

'If you're that worried about me why don't you stay at home, where you've things to attend to?'

'I have to do this. You know that and you know why.'

'Yes; yes. Your father's way. God, I wish I – we were young again; your father and me; but now, not then.'

He paused, crying. Brad, my father's twin, a memory charging an emotional spark between them. Gripping my shoulder, gulping, gasping. Something locked up escaping in sighs, flowing in his tears. Calm again, he washed his face in the river and dried it with his cap.

'Life throws such a load on some people and blows a breeze on the backs of others. I hope you'll have the breeze at your back from now on, Cormac.' He spoke as if he felt I would need that breeze.

Billy-the-bully and Christy Leahy looked smaller than I remembered, or maybe it was the way they faded into themselves behind the master's table when I walked in with Brad. They were catching up on lost time, getting tuition for Garda Síochána entrance examinations.

'You all know each other anyway,' the master announced as he took a firm hold on my hand with those long fingers, those eyes lingering on me. Billy and Christy waited for my move, then responded warmly to my handshakes. Small-talk about England and a promise to check things out for them if their plans here floundered.

The music on the fiddles, the whiskey, the master dancing

another language on the strings and in his eyes. Again the message: 'Don't waste your youth.' A plea not to turn my back on what my father stood for. It was all right to go away but the plan must be to return. Return with a purpose.

The whiskey found the dreamer in Brad as we made our way home late on that summer night. 'The master is right about some things, you know.'

I strode along beside him and waited for more.

'There seems to be change coming; he'd want you to take a hold of that change; make things happen inside it.'

We walked on among the happenings of the night; then an earlier thought became a compulsion. 'Come down to the graveyard with me, Brad.'

'The graveyard! In the dead of the night?'

'All right; you go on home. I'm going down anyway.'

He took a few steps towards home as I faced the graveyard. We paused. I handed him my fiddle.

'I'll see you in the morning,' he said.

Two graves, the repose of four people. Two graves lovingly maintained. Nearby, one newly opened; sour-sweet aroma, earth waiting to embrace flesh back to itself.

What is life? And death? Is it really the beginning it's supposed to be. Those bones over there, that skull. The buried bones and skulls of old Brad and Granny Rua; of Aunt Ellen impregnated with the seed of the Wallaces. The skeleton of my father. Bones that lived in flesh and blood, skulls that were people with eyes, brains, ears. Hearts pumping their different beats in joy, anger, sadness, fear, love, hatred.

You wouldn't tell me a lie, Granny Rua. Are you all really over there? Or is it another fable like Santa Claus and babies under cabbages or in nurses' bags?

I've slept in your bed, Granny Rua. It reminded me of so many things, of you in life, in death. Dad, what does it look like from over there? Was it worth your early call?

Or maybe there is something in Laurie's perception of our tradition, our pregnant inheritance? Does what you lived for still feel the same? Or does it have as much emotion as a tube train tracking its own lines, as much logic as a kiss with the bailiff's daughter, as much love as an ecstatic clasp to Moll Flood's hunger, to Victoria's curiosity? Of all the people, dead, enriching this acre of earth, how is it, Dad, that you still live? The dead are silent, so it is said. Silent.

At half past three in the morning, yes, there is a silence here, a waiting quiet. But you're not silent, are you, Dad, down there in your box or in that other box I keep in my belongings? No! You're not silent, nor are you dead, at least not like these others. Because your death has an echo; not the echo that fades out like lakewater smooths itself after taking back its leaping fish. No. It's the words of Brad, of the master, of almost everybody between these hills who is older than me.

Space, Dad. All those down there with you have gone from their space out here; fading memories at best, maybe dimming faces on a yellowing Mass card, a name waxing through the smoke and the snuff in the tracing of relations at wakes. Waning memories. You are more than that, drawing me into your space out here filled with challenge and expectation.

An image. No, your blazing eyes, your lean face and muscles taut as mine. Alive, on fire.

Words and aspirations, Dad. But what about the means? My means, for example, seeing that everyone including yourself seems to be looking to me to be half the man you were and utter the magic words, concoct the magic formula, beard the lion that is

Squire Wallace and free our fish and game and wildfowl and their habitats into their rightful ownership. Bring Squire Wallace down to our level, make him feel the pain of our family. For what? Who cares, Dad? Who gives a goddamn? The people who left you to die like a dog? For what, Dad?

Well, yes; rights. Land and waters of Ireland for the people of Ireland. And some of them deserve it, don't they, Dad? Some of the spineless bastards really earned their rights to it, didn't they?

Patriotism! God help us; they'd shoot their guts out their arses if they met it face to face. Yes, yes; of course there are the genuine ones setting their gardens, saving their hay and their peat, rearing their families. That's another thing, Dad; about you and Mother. How did it start? How could you keep your mind on those ideals after tasting the forbidden fruit? And how did you tell it in confession? Or did you? Because I cannot. Christ, I've been through this before.

Where are you, Dad? Surely you're not roasting in those eternal purgative flames. Surely to all that's right and good that is not possible. It's different for me: I walked myself into it and I don't love either of them. I don't know. Maybe you would have done the same.

Barely hidden under Moll's jolly demeanour, her loveless pitiable existence trapped; her heart thirsting, starving for what I could give. I gave, and she gave me a taste, no, two luscious tastes of that forbidden fruit.

That's what puzzles me, Dad. With you and Mother it must have been different; in love with each other – what am I trying to say? Yes. That taste, that experience of what is possible with a woman, a girl; that in itself also craves to be fed. It was ages, several months from that night until I met Betsy Foran in Epping, and our stolen kiss in the forest. The feel of her, so close, so giving, so wanting; I could have . . .

No; there's something about that girl; an innocence. No. And it's not because she's the bailiff's daughter.

Sorry, Granny Rua. And there's another thing, Grandad, old Brad. Your Brad is turning old with worry. This poacher tradition is turning him into a wrinkled weasel because Laurie's mind won't tune in to its dictates. Niamh and nature are twin sisters but she can't be taken inside this sanctuary of tradition.

Tradition; symbolism; patriotism. Burden! This is a new time; World War II enemies are cooperating beyond there in Europe. The world is big, changing; countries are aligning themselves under economic and monetary agreements despite the Cold War. I hope you know what's eating me. And please help me, Dad! Please.

Tiny Carmody delivered a note as I was finishing Squire's garden. It was on Highgrove Manor notepaper.

Dear Cormac MacRua

My father is away, but he requested that you call to the manor after you finish so that I can settle the account. I hope to see you presently. V. W.

'Ah, she's mellowed out a lot since she got that fall,' Tiny remarked. 'Not near the bitch she used to be; has to look after her ladyship now too, of course.'

I presented myself for settlement of the account.

'Thank you, Andrew; you might arrange to put the tea on the tray. I'll take it from there myself.' I had proceeded as indicated towards the bay window.

'As you wish, Miss Victoria.' Andrew arched one eyebrow and left.

'I – I really don't know where to begin, Cormac MacRua.'

'Cormac will do fine.'

148

'And people call me . . . '.

'I know; "Victoria" or "Miss Victoria".'

'That time, the last time . . . ', she paused, floundering. The bitch I knew could never have been flustered like this. I removed my hands from my pockets.

'I've made such mess of things; you must have a very low opinion of me.' It wasn't a question; she looked at me as if expecting me to agree.

'I wouldn't have counted the Victoria I knew as a friend.'

'It was terrible what I did, and the way I behaved that night; I can't blame you for being angry.'

So this is what was hiding in the brashness, this dignity and sensitivity. I saw something true in her eyes.

'Would it help if I said I like this Victoria and you should forget the snobbish old one and all she got up to?'

'You mean that: you could actually do that?'

Disbelief dimmed her relief.

'Of course; why not?'

'Because of . . . ' She glanced at me and looked out that bay window in the manner of her father. 'Everyone knows what's between our families, and I haven't helped.'

'What's between our families is for another time: you had nothing to do with that, Victoria.'

She allowed a smile to glimmer on her face.

'The few friends I have tend to shorten it a bit, my name I mean.'

'"Vicki", I suppose; but that wouldn't suit you at all.'

'Oh – well, what would you suggest?'

'Ria, "Ria Wallace" would fit you better, if it must be shortened. "Vicki" wouldn't have the style for a place like this.'

She blushed and grabbed my arm. 'Yes; thank you, Cormac;

I'd never have thought of that.'

She became conscious of her grip and withdrew. 'Yes; I like that.' She was searching for a way to say her next piece but I filled the space.

'There's no need to be bothering with tea; I have more gardens to do before nightfall.'

'Oh, please; you must: excuse me.'

She brought in the same tray as before but covered with an embroidered cloth. A plate of rich fruit cake diverted my hurry. Seated opposite me with the window at my back, she was more comfortable. 'You really were so gallant and discreet that day at the hunt, and . . . '

I could see that her eyes meant every word, so I extended my hand.

'Friends?' She grabbed it.

'Friends! Oh yes; oh thanks.'

'Who made the fruit cake?'

'You like it?'

'I couldn't have baked it better myself.'

She picked up the joke in my eye. A year ago it would have seemed ridiculous, impossible; but Ria Wallace laughed, and it suited her. 'I made it myself. We're supposed to learn all these things in school and college but I never took them seriously until I went back last September.'

She poured more tea and put another slice of fruit cake on my plate. 'I envy you, Cormac. I hope you don't think I'm being silly?'

'You envy me! Well, I suppose in between hunts and college, and cut off here as you are, my lifestyle would seem free and easy.'

I thought of Betsy Foran and her friends in Epping. When my mind returned to Ria there was a sadness in her eye.

'But sure you'll be off to college again in September and you'll have this August's hunt in the meantime.'

'No; I'm not going back. I got my Leaving Cert. Father is giving me responsibility for part of the house and the stables, officially from my twenty-first birthday, so that should help. And then there's Mother . . . '

'And all those extra things you learned at college.'

'Yes, I suppose – but . . . '

'The day is running away outside, Ria. I have to go. The account will be the same as always.'

'Oh dear. I'm really sorry. He'll be back on Tuesday. I'll bring it round to you then.'

Last week of the holidays. Spraying gardens in the mornings, saving hay in the afternoons, visiting at night.

Changes: Tom Flood is indeed a new man. Moll purring over baby Tomás, now ten weeks old. They joke: now that they've started there'll be no stopping them. Ria calls to settle the account. She would send me a report on the August hunt if she had my address.

Mags arranges a threehand date for Margaret and herself. Mags goes first this time; no need for instructions and indeed none given. Mags and I up against an oak tree; Margaret circling around us. Mags hoists up her skirt to squeeze my thigh between hers.

'Damn you, Mags. What do you think you're up to?'

'Shag off, Margaret; you read about it in the magazine too.' Gripping, kissing, thrusting, sighing, she squeezes out her climax.

Later when I am walking Margaret home she strides ahead of me, head down, arms folded.

'I've had enough of this sulking; I'm heading home to the Glens.'

Her head comes up but no comment. I turn for home. A field later I hear and feel the running steps. 'Sorry, Cormac; I don't know what's wrong with me.'

'You're supposed to be trying things out from a magazine I haven't seen, so how would I know?'

'It's not that, Cormac. I want – I don't want – I can't take it when you're that way – with someone else.'

'Heck, Margaret, it's only fun. The two of you made the arrangement, and Mags obviously enjoyed her bit.'

'Yes. I know; sorry. But it's my turn now; and they weren't standing up, in the magazine.'

TWELVE

'Australia! My God that's a fair wee distance he's putting between us.'

'Australia?' the murmur ran among the veterans nodding agreement with Ethel Gibbons.

'It's an offer I got from one of the British equitation team; she wants me to travel with the horses as farrier and groom.'

'My God, that could take ages; months and months and little enough we see of you as it is. And what about your plans for that diploma? Abandoning us, everything, to run off to the belly of the world with a pack o' horses, and a woman?'

'Madness! he's gone pure mad,' some nodded.

'Ah give the wee lad a chance,' old Derry Joe teased. 'Yous are only jealous, wishin' youse were young like him again yourselves.'

'And what age, may I ask, is this woman? Where did she rise out of?' Ethel seemed concerned.

'Older than you anyway, her son lectures in the college and she hunts out in Phillips estate.'

Joy's request that I adopt British citizenship to facilitate team and transport administration made the whole idea impracticable. Joy was my mentor, the horsy lady from Phillips Manor and Epping, who had long since outgrown the appropriateness of such a name.

'Surely you can take up your studies after you get home next year? Though what practical use they have in this business beats me. Veterinary I could understand. And what's a year at your age, for goodness sake?'

'It's not the time; more a question of priorities, and principle.'

'Priorities and principle! In a stable? Good Lord, what next?' Though in a state of impatient agitation she still observed my work on her horse's hooves.

'This stable, this yard, this estate are only a phase for me, Madam; just keeping my hand in and working my way to better things.'

'It's dangerous for a farrier to look up; could hit the quick.'

I pretended not to have received her figurative message.

'Did you actually use the word "principle"?'

'Would *you* become an Irish citizen, Madam?'

'Perish the thought; what an impossible suggestion!'

'That works both ways; so you'd better look around for a British citizen to accompany your Irish horses down under.' I continued applying my homemade solution.

Her reply, if it came, should reflect her mind.

'That solution absolutely stinks. I don't suppose there's any point in asking what's in it?'

'When I'm ready I'll let you know.'

'You do that; and I'll see what I can do to satisfy your "priorities and principle".'

She couldn't understand what I meant. My focus now was on Sir W. H. Wallace, Bart.

Coopers Common was an extension of Phillips Estate in an area of Epping that was essentially old England. Danny Farr's smithy would have fitted in perfectly. Uncle Peter's stonecraft would have earned him a fortune in respect and cash. Brad would have loved the game and the fish in the brooks, though it took me a while to coax the trout on to my fingers. He would have been fascinated by the range of fly-fishing gear used by the anglers and would have made easier money than toiling with his machinery by providing trout for boasting anglers who 'lost' the big one on the day.

Betsy and her nurse colleagues loved the sunny common, baring what they dared to worship the sun god in that lovely summer of 1959. Ethel Gibbons made an arrangement with the Green Line to transport her veterans and staff to the area for a week's holidays, staying at Magdalen Hospital where Betsy worked.

Betsy had a boyfriend, a young local police constable who adored her. The greater Jeff's worship the more indifferent Betsy's reaction. The arrival of Ethel and her veterans was a godsend, coinciding with Jeff's week on nights. Betsy wanted to talk privately out in the common at night. That's the way it would have to be done. And what's more she would have to have a drink in Fiddler's Hamlet to work up to what she had to say. Jeff had introduced her to vodka and she liked the effect.

Later, on a secluded knoll, we chatted. She wanted to be a nurse more than anything else.

And then she came to the point. 'Jeff wants me to do it with him, Cormac.'

'Damn it, Betsy; you're not that stupid surely?'

'It's not that stupid. A lot of the girls do it with their boyfriends. It's quite safe you know, with precautions.'

'Precautions?'

'Ah, Cormac, don't pretend to be so innocent.'

'Oh I know what they are; but you and Jeff?'

'Well, you see, I like him. He's very good to me: taking me to shows and films and dinner and everything.'

'And you want to give him something back? I don't believe you.'

'You're annoyed with me, aren't you?'

'Surprised.'

'Look, Jeff has never done it and neither have I, though it was a close thing the night I slept over with him.'

'You slept with him?'

'Well, his mother was away and I was to have the guest room. I slept there before and everything was fine.'

I waited for the real Betsy to speak.

'I can't see myself marrying him, though he has asked me that too. But he's good company. Oh but he gets so agitated when I don't let him go all the way.'

'It's wrong. You know that, don't you?'

'Is it really that wrong, Cormac? Do you mean to tell me you haven't done it?'

I cuddled her to me. The dry grass still held the heat of the day.

'You must have done it? Tell me about it, Cormac, please.'

'If Jeff loves you enough, he'll wait.'

'But he says if I love him enough, I'll do it.'

'That's the problem, isn't it?'

'What?'

'Doing it: It! It! As if it was learning to swim. 'Tis supposed to be part of the special magic between two people and I don't see any magic between you and Jeff.'

She was making it difficult for me to mean what I was trying to say.

'He wouldn't pester you about doing it when you don't want to, if he loves you as much as he says he does.'

'But I do – want to, or to try it anyway.'

Now I was confused. I laid back and rested my head in my hands. I could visualise Betsy, legs clasped around Jeff, thrusting, panting. No, not Betsy, not with him.

'Do you feel the magic between you and me, Cormac?'

She was leaning over me, opening the buttons of my shirt.

'Don't tempt me, Betsy.'

'Your mother and father did it, didn't they?'

I threw her from me. I couldn't speak. Mother and Father swirling around in my head, Betsy a schoolchild back in the Glens, taunting: 'If your father was such a great man, why didn't he marry your mother?'

I run but they stay with me. Mother defiled; no; Father the defiler; no. No! They were in love, deeply, beautifully in love; no pestering, no 'it'; true love.

Four letters await me on my return with Ethel Gibbons and her care to the Veterans' Home.

The Glens

16 August 1959

My dear Cormac

We are worried about you here. No word from you for over a month. Is something wrong? You must write please as soon as you get this letter, a few lines will do.

We are all fine here, though Brad was very angry when you couldn't come to help even for a week. I know you'd have come if you could. The children all miss you. Laurie has taken to the stonework with Uncle Peter like he was born to it, and he can manage the spraying machine and repair it – no bother. Niamh is a great help and the master is very pleased with her schoolwork. I think she misses you the most.

Mary and the twins want to know if you're coming for Christmas and what you're going to bring them. Granma is not so good these times. She's back home in Heather Hill now and is very slow to leave the bed. In fact Breda has to coax her to get up. Having lost her speech again doesn't help. Breda is great with her though. Peter and Danny are fine. You'll lose track of your first cousins if you don't come home soon.

Lots of people ask about you when I meet them at Mass, and the master wants you to write to him.

So please write soon and be sure to have something to say to Brad. He needs a bit of humouring these times, and I think you know what it's all about.

Until I hear from you, lots of love,
Always your loving Mother and family

Highgrove Manor
17/8/59

Dear Cormac

I hope this finds you well because your young brother was giving nothing away when he was up here last week.

I promised to tell you about the hunt. It was a bit of a non-event really because of the long spell of dry weather making the ground so hard. Brad MacRua did a great job in raising the fox as usual but we got nowhere near him as the horses were understandably reticent. So no silly accidents on this occasion.

I mentioned that Father gave me responsibility for part of the house and the stables. Progress is very slow because of Mother. Most of the time she's ill, and when she's up and about she criticises everything I do. So the entire household has been subject to her whims in one way or another for months now.

I know it's a long way ahead but next year is my twenty-second birthday. You made it so easy for me to talk to you that day ages ago when we spoke here that I feel I can call you a true friend. We shook hands on it, didn't we? So perhaps you could arrange your next summer holidays for the August hunt and join me for the party I'm sure Father will organise. The twenty-second birthday is the big one for girls in our family, so with a bit of luck Father may even splash out on a debutante ball.

Incidentally I have cooled things with my beau, not that they were ever very hot. It's just that we seem to have grown apart. Of course Mother thinks he's a darling.

He's nice but so is jelly. Not the sort I want to reach out to: male, but not a man; you know what I mean. Sorry! I shouldn't be boring you with personal matters.

Now that I have written to you again perhaps you could write to me and tell me about all the exciting things that keep you away from home for so long.

I remain,

Your friend,

Ria

Benmore

13/8/59

Dear Cormac

For some reason you haven't got around to answering my previous letters, and then not coming home this summer when I really wanted to talk to you.

I would like your advice on what I should do about a career. I have a choice between the civil service or teaching. I have to make up my mind in two weeks so please write and tell me what you think.

I always remember that last night before you went away. I never realised a boy could make a girl feel so good. I dream about you all the time and I hope you come back soon, even for a little while.

Everyone at the rambling house sends their regards, and Mags keeps asking if I have heard from you. She's still knitting and getting the magazines from her cousin, but she doesn't show them to me anymore.

Cormac my darling, please write straight away and advise me what to do,

Your always everloving
Margaret
XXXX

Dear young Cormac

Letter writing is something I try to avoid as it reminds me too much of the classroom. I gather that you haven't wasted too much ink yourself in the last two years. I have no doubt that you're knocking a fair old tune out of life over there but don't forget completely about us or about ultimately getting back here to make a few overdue adjustments.

The night you called on your last holidays you surprisingly offered to help Billy and Christy should they fail to pass those entrance exams. Despite my best efforts they have indeed failed, and repeatedly. They asked me if you could find out what the entry requirements are to the police force over there.

To be perfectly honest what you should do is get the names of a few contractors. They'd handle basic machinery with a bit of training. It would be up to themselves after that. You might make a few enquiries and get back to me because we should get them started somewhere, now that they are so inclined to do something for themselves.

Meanwhile keep up the music.
Yours in life.
(Master) Pat O'Donnell

Dear Mother, Brad, brothers and sisters

Sorry you got the impression I had forgotten you and how important you all are in my life. And sorry, Brad, that I couldn't manage a few weeks to help out this summer. There were many times when I thought of you and how you would fit into the scheme of things over here.

I hope you are all keeping well as indeed I am. The way things stand at present I'm not sure exactly when I'll get home but I hope to take a break at Christmas.

There seems to be no end to the opportunities over here. Study takes a lot of time, not that it's difficult but we are left to set our own limits. There's still time to play and teach a little music; there are more young ones thirsting for our music and culture here than at home.

The money enclosed is what I made over a month or so for pointing out the good trout runs to anglers in the rivers and streams they call brooks here. There should be enough there to buy a young cob to give Stepper a rest, to give the children a half-crown each and have a few pounds left over for yourselves.

It looked for a while like I was off to Australia to look after a few horses for a Commonwealth competition. However I'll just lead the horses on board and settle them in the ocean liner in Southampton next week.

I have to stay here to register for my final year. And, Brad, I haven't forgotten family matters. In fact they occupy more of my plans each month.

I have a few more letters to answer, so I'll close for now.

Yours always,

Cormac

Dear Master Pat

Thanks for your letter just received, and glad to see you haven't changed. I've just written home and kept an extra drop of ink for this short note.

You should get the lads to learn to drive something, even a tractor, before they come over. It would help too if they learned a little of the geography of the place such as where the main cities are in relation to each other and the layout of the greater London area. My own sketch of a map is enclosed. When they're ready, make them write letting me know their arrangements. I'll meet them in Euston and fix them up with accommodation and a start. That's enough ink for you for now. Music is going great. Kind regards always,

Cormac MacRua

Dear Ria

Thanks for your letter just received. I obviously didn't miss much at the hunt.

Your mother is probably finding it difficult to get used to you around the manor all the time. Why don't you play along with her, about how you are trying to maintain her style and standards and so on. Make her feel good and she mightn't be such a blight on you.

Thanks for inviting me to your special birthday and of course I would like to be there, though there are some who would not approve. It's too early for me to promise as it depends on how related matters develop.

Don't worry about the beau. If you're not longing for the sound of his wheels don't hitch yourself to his wagon. You were a most obnoxious bitch when I met you first but the real you seems to be breaking through now. While most of the men in your social class are self-centred stuck-up toffs there's sure to be one out there who deserves you. I'm no expert, but people old enough to know tell me that you'll tingle when that time comes.

It's a long way ahead but if I don't see you in the meantime, happy birthday.
Your friend,
Cormac

Veterans' Home,
London SW1
21/8/59

Dear Margaret

The reason I haven't answered your letters is I didn't have much to say. Well done in achieving your options.

I don't think I'm the best person to advise you but for what it's worth you might be more suited to the civil service or the bank than to teaching. It's just a feeling I have. Don't ask me to analyse it.

It's always great to hear from you. I look forward to getting together next time I'm home. Meanwhile good luck in your choice of career.
Your friend,
Cormac

Southampton was huge. Ocean liners and cargo ships dwarfed yachts, ferries and trawlers. Joy maintained a stiff civility as I led the horses on board and settled them in the luxury of their deck covered in a mixture of sand, straw, bark and sawdust. I would miss them – the horses, not Joy. Her training programme had them shining and frisky and my solution was working. Not a sign of a crack in their hooves.

'So how stand your "priorities and principle" now?'

'No change.'

'Bravado; you're as sick as a tub of guts.'

'Goodbye, Madam; and best of luck with my friends.'

'Stubborn.'

She was right. I was sick, but not sick enough to renege on everything I stood for. Ethel Gibbons was triumphant. She needed my help to have her Veterans' Home fully recognised under the health acts.

Veteran women also had to be accommodated and she needed someone who could read her mind and what should be in her mind. Pay? Where would she get money to pay?

'Would you get paid if you were headed to Australia?'

'Yes, I would.'

'But we have to do something soon about our wee problem, Cormac. Refusing people who did their service in the war can't be tolerated, not even from the high and mighty Department of Health.'

Yes, this was the type of fight that appealed to me; a practice run before confronting Squire.

'Come on; I need a few hands to help me measure up the buildings and grounds, and then we'll put down on paper everything we want and estimate the cost. That should get things started.'

The first women peers had been introduced to the House of Lords on 21 October 1958. Empire Day was to be renamed Commonwealth Day in December. A campaign with the veterans themselves as allies would surely find a nerve in numbed official conscience. Men and women who had served their country were now mere statistics left to die off out of sight. Ethel managed to get a block of tickets to Convent Garden and made sure the Press were tuned up.

They obliged with headlines such as 'World War Veterans enjoy the Ballet'. What a night that was! The way they interpreted Beethoven and his masters, Mozart and Haydn; the Symphony in E Flat Major; the Romance in F Major.

'Veterans without a Home; Country without a Soul,' and 'Well done, Lady Peers: we were with you all the way.' The headlines aroused an unwary public. Officialdom responded with a scheme of empty words. Ethel was too close to the human reality to be taken in. 'Surplus huts no longer in service in army barracks could be erected in the ground,' officialdom said. 'It would be like old times for the veterans; they could live in small groups and yet enjoy the facilities of the Home.'

If the huts were unfit for use by the army they were equally unfit for the veterans, we pointed out.

'You have the plans; everything on a plate for you. Now get off your wee shiners and give us the money to build,' Ethel challenged.

Invisible headlines from the past came to taunt me. In the quiet of the night, in moments of victory with Ethel, the words, 'Ready to fight everybody's battle but your own. What about the squire?' cast doubts on my motivation.

Home for the shortest possible Christmas visit to update that space in my heart marked 'family'. Home just in time to join Brad for the water bailiff's funeral. He would have been proud of the dignity his daughter Betsy brought to the occasion. A welcome chance to appreciate Brad through changed eyes. Listening, questioning: what was life really like over there?

Were my plans still on course for coming back? he wondered. The children; still no sign of a new Brad. What about Niamh?

No; it would have to be a son.

He had two men working with him now; come to him in the strangest circumstances, two former classmates from that night we were up at the master's. They were thinking of going to England and wanted to learn how to handle machinery. Good learners they were, once they got the hang of it. And with so much work around they stayed on.

Mother: wouldn't Ethel Gibbons love her easy way of blending office and family duties while seeming to have plenty of time to chat to visitors or customers! We talk.

'He was about your age when I met him first, Cormac.'

'I often think about him, you know; about you all when I'm over there but in a different way about him.'

'You have his box, haven't you?' She took me by surprise. I thought she had forgotten all about it.

'How did you know?'

'I'm your mother. We've been through a lot together, you and me.'

'Brad seems a bit easier in himself.'

'He'd want to be; took him a long time to accept you were gone, like that saying in the Bible "about your father's business"?'

'I often wonder how you fit the two of them into your heart?'

'They're twins. You manage it, don't you, as a son? They have their own place in their own time.' I nodded.

'Is there anyone in your heart?'

'No one in sole possession anyway. Too much happening, I suppose.'

'What's happening is what you make happen.'

'I know – from my father's box.'

'We had a party when we were eighteen; a picnic party at the top of Heather Hill.'

I waited.

'Lemonade was a great treat and hard to get but he got two bottles. Scones we had with it. I swapped a piece of smoked salmon he gave me to get the currants.'

'Who else was there?'

'It was just for us, Cormac, and me. It was lovely, just lovely.' Joy sparkled in her eyes. 'You'd better go to bed, Cormac. You'll have to be up again in a few hours for early Mass.'

'I'm going when you're going.' I held her, the most precious person on earth. No need for words.

I'm not the only one on holidays. Margaret Wally is at Mass, home from her new job in the Department of Education. She has matured – a woman now. Niamh nudges me. Betsy Foran is coming into our seat.

Fr Lynch encourages his congregation to join in the Christmas hymns. From a few seats back the master's baritone rings strong and true. A little closer, perhaps two seats behind us, a tuneful soprano. A touch of sadness lilting in her voice. I should know that voice but cannot place it. Niamh and Betsy join me in impromptu harmony.

> Once in royal David's city
> Stood a lowly cattle shed,
> Where a mother laid her baby
> In a manger for his bed:
> Mary was that mother mild,
> Jesus Christ her little child.

What a time to think of this. Joseph accepted Jesus as a son even though he wasn't the father. Brad accepted me likewise but at an implied price.

The atmosphere was one of all-embracing reverent love: Fr Lynch's Latin invocations; Laurie leading two other altar boys responding in a rattling chant; the bells; the aroma of smells rising in body heat; the jingle of copper coins in the collection boxes.

A whisper from Betsy. 'When are you going back, Cormac?'

'Day after tomorrow, the twenty-seventh.'

'As soon as that?'

'Have to; Ethel has so much to do.'

'Can I come with you, please. I couldn't face it on my own this time?'

'Of course. I'll see you to the nurses' home.'

'Trust you, Cormac. Happy Christmas.'

'Happy Christmas, Betsy.'

Voices fully warmed up; 'Hark the Herald Angels . . . ' swells through the church as the Mass ends.

The soprano is coming through more strongly. It's Ria.

Joyful all ye nations rise
Join the triumph of the skies . . .

She smiles. I make a wish for her. She deserves, needs somebody good, someone who would treat her to lemonade and scones on a sunny hilltop. 1960 maybe.

Murmuring shuffles out into the yard to a cascade of goodwill. Greetings, intermingling everywhere; then women slipping away to pot-roasting goose or lamb.

Ria's two-handed handshake. 'It's great you could get home; you must give us a call. Father has heard so much about you from Phillips.'

'Barely a family visit, Ria; getting the early train on the 27th and I'm going to Heather Hill tomorrow.'

'Of course! I understand. Your letters are so good. I often read them at night. You'll write. Promise!'

'I'll write, Ria. Happy Christmas, and I hope something nice happens for you in the new year.'

'Christmas kiss?'

'M-m-m.'

'Keep one for me!' Margaret Wally joins in. Ria waves goodbye.

'Going back so soon! Can you fit in the rambling house tomorrow night, even?'

'If you'll be there, I'll be there.'

'Terrific. Happy Christmas.'

It was a white Christmas on Heather Hill. Brad stayed home in the Glens but gave me a side of smoked salmon for each household, subsequently exchanged for rabbits from Nellie and ducks from Breda. Children, cousins revelling in the snow. Granpa Healy's old hat tops off a cooperative snowman.

More goose, duck, ham; poteen-laden plum pudding; sharing again the news from London. Absent folk remembered; glasses raised to the new year.

'Agus go mbeirimíd beo ar an am seo aris.'

'And may we all be alive when this time comes around again.'

An asbestos lean-to offered much needed extra space at the rambling house. A gramophone horn attached to the fiddle amplified the sound and Mags-the-well beat out the rhythm on the *bodhrán*. Christy Leahy had slipped into the role of boyfriend to Mags.

'That's a fine jumper you knitted the boyfriend, Mags. Is he worth it?'

'Ah sure he's a bit shy, but he'll be learning. What are you up to yourself?'

'Starting back in the morning on the early train.'

169

'You know well that's not what I mean.'

Later, at Margaret Wally's gate, 'You'd do very well in Dublin, Cormac, if you came back.'

'When I come back it'll be around here, I'm sure.'

'There's nothing around here for you now. You'd never settle.'

I couldn't tell her the plan I was plotting.

'You like Dublin, do you?'

'Yes; great life in the place, considering.'

'I'm delighted for you.'

We paused and faced each other at arm's length.

'Do you mind if I ask you something, Cormac?'

'Try me.'

'Is there something between Victoria Wallace and you?'

'She's a friend. I've grown quite fond of her.'

'You write to her; I heard her saying it.'

'I write to my close friends whenever I can.'

'Well, at least I'm a close friend.'

'You're a different kind of close friend; this kind.'

Back with Ethel and the veterans I keep my promises to write: Mother and Brad, a note for each of the children; the master, Margaret Wally, Ria Wallace.

Betsy Foran has delayed reaction to her father's death. Her boyfriend cannot understand it. I can, so we walk and talk in Epping Forest twice a week. She cries. I hold her, soothe her. How long can I keep doing this? Why do I want to keep doing it, with so much clamouring for space in my life? Diploma exams, Veterans' Home, contact with home, Phillips estate, the mellow aftertaste of Margaret Wally, music. My father's business.

THIRTEEN

'Keep going like this and you'll be ancient by twenty-five,' Ethel Gibbons observed on the night of my twenty-first birthday. The veterans had conspired with Betsy to arrange a return visit from the nurses' home as a surprise party.

'But I don't feel tired, Ethel; there's so much to be done.'

'And there's no one else to do it, of course!'

'Look who's talking.'

"Tis different for me. I won't wake up one morning wondering where my youth has gone.'

'Did you do anything special when you were twenty-one?'

'How many girlfriends have you?'

'Nothing serious: two – three maybe.'

'Good for you. I spent that birthday running after a wee creep that wasn't worth it.'

'I was wondering if there was somebody in your life?'

'There's many a wee one would envy my situation in a house full of men and you as my adopted son.'

'And you, how do you feel?'

'Haven't time to be thinking that way. But you've a bit of thinking to do with two girlfriends back home and one over here that I know of.'

'I haven't anyone here in the way you mean, and definitely only one at home with a romantic side to the friendship.'

'Maybe that's the way you see it. But your friend Betsy had a persistent phone caller last night, a wee lad that eventually identified himself as her boyfriend; and do you know what she did?'

'What?'

'Asked me to tell him her boyfriend was here.'

'He won't like that.'

'He isn't supposed to.' What a great mother she would make.

'And then there's all these letters; one a month from the young lady of the manor and a bit more often from the romantic one in Dublin,' she continued.

'Ria is just a friend. I feel strange about that sometimes. I'll be fighting with her father soon.'

'And you like her too much to do that?'

'I'm leading her on, to be honest. We're on different sides. I'll have to explain that to her.'

'When?'

'After the exams. June; I'll do it in June.'

Examinations: so many types of tests.

Dublin
1/5/60

Dear Cormac

Summer approaches at last. I've been looking forward to it so much, hoping that we can be together a lot more over a longer holiday, especially after our far too short date at Christmas.

I realise of course that you are preoccupied with your exams coming up soon and your work for that very interesting lady in Veterans' Home but please let me know when and if you plan to get home during the summer. I want to be sure to arrange my holidays for the same time. If you are not coming home I will take my holidays over there so that we can have some time together. From my point of view August would be a good time.

Let me know as soon as you can, please, so that I can make arrangements here with the section supervisor.

Love Margaret xxxxx

The Glens

5/5/60

My dear Cormac

Thanks for your letters and money for the children at Easter. We're glad to know you're well, as this leaves us all here. You haven't mentioned anything about coming this summer. Brad has his own reasons for asking, though he assures me 'tis not to make a slave out of you. He says what he wants you for is much more important than work.

Niamh is supervising the correspondence from the children, except Laurie who spends whatever spare time he can with Uncle Peter. 'Tis true what Peter says about him; with only a small bit of help he put up a fine stone wall down at the end of the yard. Brad thinks better of him now after that.

I was surprised when Victoria Wallace came over talking to me after Sunday Mass, though she has been very friendly of late. It seems her mother is on her last legs and there's nothing the doctors can do for her. As cranky as a bag of cats I believe. Victoria's face shows signs of it too. She asked me if I could help with nursing a couple of mornings a week because her mother has frightened off the nurses sent by the doctors. I've mixed feelings about it but 'tis hard to refuse a plea for help like that. The poor girl obviously hasn't had a proper night's sleep in ages. Anyway that's probably of no interest to you, though she was asking about you.

You'll write soon, won't you?

Love and good luck always.

Mammy and Brad

(Children's letters enclosed.)

Dear Cormac

   Please excuse the rush and the brevity. Thanks for your last letter, helpful as usual.

   Before I forget it, father wants to speak to you about doing a survey of the estate as you did for cousin Phillips. He will pay, of course. You know the way he is; once he decides on something he won't rest until it's done. The last thing I need at present is agitation, so maybe you could write and set your time and terms and so on.

   Mother is such a bother, possessing me totally now. As she is such a nag anyway it's hard to know how much she's actually suffering. I've moved a chaise-longue *to her bedroom to be near her as much as possible. Sometimes when I give her the medication she spits it back at me. O God, I cannot tell you the unspeakable dark wish that boils up inside me sometimes.*

   Write me a long letter please, Cormac, or a short one I can read over and over. And please, please give me a little of your time soon.
Your fond friend,
Ria

Shortly after I had read this letter, Ria's telegram arrived with news of her mother's death. Happy release.

Dear Sir W. H. Wallace

   Please accept my sincere sympathies on the recent death of your wife after such a long illness.

   I have already written to Victoria, who has advised me of your wish to complete a survey of your estate. Before we do business at that level however there is a matter of principle which I have to address, a matter which we spoke about in the context of my father when you first invited me into your drawing-room. It has been my intention to pursue this matter with you as soon as I was qualified to do so. It helps that you now recognise those qualifications.

The issue is the question of the title vested in Highgrove Estate over the gaming and fishing rights in the barony roundabout, particularly Hare Mountain and the Glens. The title has made criminals by implication of my family for exercising rights which would be taken for granted here, say to the smallholders in Essex or indeed by most farmers at home. There are rights vested in Highgrove Estate therefore which should have passed with their land to the smallholders under the spirit of the Wyndham Act of 1903 as applied to the 1937 Agreement. The fact that others exercised the same options as your father at the time does not make it right.

I believe that negotiation and not confrontation is the way to address this. You will agree that justice delayed is justice denied. I do not believe that you would want to fall at this final hurdle, so I am serving notice that I want to address this matter as soon as possible.

Business is business, as General Phillips constantly states. The survey can be completed parallel with the above negotiations. I would suggest the second half of August this year as a suitable time. A schedule specifying scope and cost is enclosed for your perusal.
Yours sincerely
Cormac MacRua

Twelve days of examinations ahead but at least the practicals and field work are already secured. To revise or not to revise.

The box, my father's box in my consciousness. I felt compelled to open it even though familiar with each item and word it contained. It was 1.30 a.m. Each hair stood on the tingling in my skin. I spread the contents on my table. Letters to Squire Wallace, one reply (1938), letter to Registry of Deeds with a reply, a penny, halfpenny and farthing, a cross and five beads of an old rosary, a miraculous medal, letters to my mother, typically ending:

I keep thinking of you and thanking the good Lord for the good fortune of your love.

Until I see you here's all my love.

Forever yours

Cormac

Highgrove Manor
25 June 1960

Dear Cormac MacRua,

Your letter of 30 May refers. Your expression of sympathy is appreciated.

I am not sure that I welcome the contents, though I should not be surprised with them, coming from you.

First of all to show that I bear no ill feeling towards you but rather admire what you have achieved, I accept your specifications and cost structure for the survey. I want you to start at the time set out, if not earlier. A booking deposit of 10% is enclosed in confirmation.

The matter of Highgrove Estate surrendering what has been its rights for generations is something I will not do. Consider my position.

If I were to surrender those rights, what then? Gradually surrender my lands also? What about the tradition of the hunt? I would have no difficulty with you or your uncle Brad having concessions on taking fish or game within reason, which may indeed be recognising what is the actual position in any case. But what then? If I surrender to you, others will demand more, thereby eroding a system which has worked for generations.

To compare East Kerry with Essex is not comparing like with like. You will have noticed that people over there hold the law in higher regard than do people here. So it's not a practical concession in that very context.

I am however open to discussion on any injustices you perceive within the system as it stands, and remain,
Yours truly
W. H. Wallace, Bart.

Naked reality. The dream suspended in my father's sleep awakens to impervious dawn. His life, his death has changed nothing at the manor. No; not there. But what was romantic duty to his dream now surges in anger through his genes in my veins.

MacRua against the Wallace Manor. Squire, sitting on history. My head, ready, wondering what's going on in my heart. See-saw of indecision in my personal life, with Margaret Wally as *see* and Betsy Foran as *saw*. Betsy knows about Margaret. She has no difficulty with that. I have. Margaret does not know of the relationship that has developed with Betsy and I don't want her to know. She wouldn't understand. While I have no formal commitment to Margaret, her place in my heart nags that I am cheating. Betsy has followed me on holidays.

The drawing-room of Highgrove was magnificent, Ria's touch everywhere. The room was alive, drawing in sunlight and giving it back in a blend of colour.

'There's an office set up for you upstairs; used to be a bedroom. The bed is still in it actually should you like to stay over any night. Things might be a bit crowded at home with all the children.'

Squire's offer was placed with strategic perfection. No mention of our correspondence or of the business he knew consumed me.

177

'Very considerate of you, Squire; thanks. I may indeed avail of your offer.'

'Don't thank me.' He inclined his head towards the kitchen. 'Thank her. I'll never understand them. Most who come here are attended to by the servants. She supervises them of course, not that they need much of that nowadays. Then you arrive and she must look after you personally.'

'They're probably off, or busy at something else.'

'Off? Not one of them; preparing for her ball actually. Two days' time. Oh, damn near forgot: she wants you to be her escort; says she's mentioned it to you already. Making a once-off occasion of it so it's up to me, it seems, to invite her beau.'

'I'll be glad to. Nothing too formal, I hope?'

'Well, formal dress of course, especially for you. A few bits in my younger wardrobe would fit, I'm sure.'

Ria returned bearing a tray.

'So that's all settled, I take it?' the squire asked.

'Yes; I'm looking forward to it.'

'So now, Victoria, that's done. You heard what he said.'

'Oh, thanks, Cormac; you don't know how much that means.' A kiss conveyed her appreciation.

'He's travelling light though, so you'll have to go through the wardrobes to dress him up.'

'It's all right, everything is selected; just leave it to me, Father.'

While we take our snack, every word of Squire's letter crosses my mind, a letter which changed little from that written to my father in 1938. I try to reopen the matter.

'About our business . . . '

'Oh, yes. Better be getting along, hadn't we? What will you be needing?' He dodged the grapple.

'Ordnance Survey maps and a horse. I'll spend my first few

days on a detailed examination of each field. I may as well leave my case in the office.'

'I'll attend to that,' Ria intervened. While she was gone: 'There was also the business I raised in our correspondence. Maybe if you ride with me we can talk?'

'You don't give up easily, do you? Very well, we can talk. I'll arrange the horses.'

I set the terms of our discussion for the first day. Squire had given his point of view. Now I would give mine. He agrees. It is a fencing-match. Occasionally he drops his guard.

'Twenty-two she'll be. She told you that, I presume. Time for her to be getting a beau for real. No interest in anyone we have introduced to her in the last few years.'

'I thought she had a fiancé at one stage.'

'Oh, him? No. I'm thinking of someone fit to be her husband, a man with what it takes to run this place.'

'Has she mentioned anybody?'

'No.' He led the way upwards. I joined him at a gateway.

'I had hoped to semi-retire in a year or two but without someone acceptable to her to take my place . . . ' He trailed off and led the way along the slopes. I could see the patches of erosion.

'Phillips tells me you have a way of arresting and reversing this erosion.'

'I'll work on a few options to find the best way.'

'What age are you?'

'Twenty-one.'

'There must be some mistake, surely?'

'You can easily count it back to 1939, or the events of July 1938 if you wish.'

'Point taken.'

I decide to play another card. I steer King Henry to a point

179

overlooking Benmore Valley and the Glens. Squire follows and observes: 'Marvellous vista, isn't it? There's nowhere in the world can beat this in my mind.'

I can see he means it. I nudge him back to my reality.

'I wonder how one of those farmers out there, looking for a husband for his daughter, would explain to him that the fish and game belong to someone else?'

'It's been a long day. I must be getting back.'

I watch him go. King Henry moves to follow but I hold him. The view holds me.

I pick out our holding, bold in its greenery, oats ripening to gold, before surrendering to the mountain heather and thyme. The smells are different now: the bitter scent of hunger is no more. Off to my right the sun warms the Dingle sky in the glow of its redness as it prepares to dip beyond the Atlantic for the night. The same sun in the morning will light the gentle slopes of Heather Hill away to my left where the talents of his maternal grandfather are already breaking out in young Laurie MacRua.

Later, after stabling King Henry, I stop. I know I am standing on the spot where my father died, where he was killed. I squat down, look around. Dreams, revelations flash. Anger: why; what did you think you were doing drowning your courage in concocted spirits? And what am I doing here with your killer, you ask. Can you not see my strategy?

I notice the ivy-covered building between the stables and the cattle stalls. I peep inside. It's the dairy, about the size of our house in the Glens. Cool from the ivy and a water system I cannot quite see, its layout is even better than Phillips'. The milk tanks, separator, butter churn and cheese tubs, all in a cool world of their own.

'You can stay the night, any night you like?' Ria assures me after dinner as we sit and talk in the office.

'Thanks; I will, but I must get home too. No point in being this close to them if I can't be among them as often as I can.'

'Betsy Foran dropped by today. I believe you're very good friends now.'

'Well, after her father died – over there she was lonely.'

'I know what you mean. Anyone else in your life?'

'Margaret Wally.'

'Oh yes. I saw her with you at Christmas.' Her smile could not hide something lonesome in her eyes.

'It must be strange now that your mother is gone?'

'Yes, but somehow better; for the first time I can think of being myself.'

'You've done wonders with the house, the manor.'

'Thanks. I'm glad you're impressed.' She smiled.

'Ria, I know that things were difficult for you with your mother's demands but is there any sign at all of that man you've been dreaming about?'

'The one to appreciate what I really am?'

'You're using my own words again.' She looked at me and walked around behind my chair.

'You don't mind being my escort Wednesday night, Cormac?'

'I'm looking forward to it, and I promise you a little surprise.'

'Really! You really mean that, don't you?'

'Trust me, Ria; you'll have a great night.'

'You'll stay that night, won't you? You must.'

'How could I refuse a debutante on her birthday?'

Later that night, with Margaret, my mind is pulled back to Highgrove Manor. The squire riding away from my question; Ria; Ria. Something about her. That brashness, that arrogance of a few years ago all chipped away. Something else grown in its place under a candid shyness. Something . . .

'Cormac?' She shook me.

'Sorry, Margaret; were you saying something?'

'Was I saying something! Giving out my speech about the pattern night at the rambling house and your mind over in London or somewhere.'

'Sorry. When is it?'

'When is it? You didn't even hear that! Wednesday night.'

'Sorry. Wednesday night is out.'

'What! I arrange my holidays to fit in with yours and the best night in it is out?'

'I have an engagement at Highgrove Manor. It's a matter of honour.'

'A matter of honour? You mean a duel or something.'

'At a remove, perhaps it is: a duel, a rematch; yes.'

'That wasn't meant to be serious. Can't you come afterwards?'

'No. Wednesday night, all night is out.'

'Cormac, is there someone else?'

'Tomorrow night I'm meeting Betsy Foran. I promised to go through her father's things with her.'

'Oh, thanks for telling me. And what am I supposed to do? Tuesday night my boyfriend meets Betsy, the daughter of the bailiff he hated. Wednesday night is mystery night all night at the manor under the roof of the man that killed his father.'

'I have things to do, Margaret, promises to finish.'

'What about your promises to me?'

'What promises?'

'What promises! These holidays for example. I've waited eight long months to get together with you?'

'I'll take you to the pictures in Ballybo, Friday night.'

'What about Thursday night?'

'Family; I promised to stay at home that night.'

'I don't know what's got into you, Cormac; you're so complicated.'

The bailiff's diaries were a written obsession with two generations of Brad MacRuas. Betsy busied herself with something roasting in the pot while I read of close calls, vigils near our house for signs of movement, decoy chases, and, not surprisingly, the ulcers which tended to flare up after the close calls.

'How faithful is a dog?' he wrote in frustration after that night at the waterfall in the upper Glens. In 1948 I got my first mention as 'the boy', later 'his boy'.

Brad would be interested in these diaries and could be trusted not to breach their confidentiality.

'What am I going to do with this place, Cormac?'

'That's like asking what you're going to do with yourself?'

'You're right; in a way, it is.' Betsy looked downcast.

'So what are you going to do with yourself?'

'Look who's asking! I'm waiting for you.'

'Please don't do that, Betsy. My head can't get any bearings on my heart at the moment.'

'Things only get confused when you come home. Everything will be fine when we get back.'

'Jeff is still waiting for you over there. He loves you.'

'He's too wishy-washy; I don't love him.'

'I don't love you.'

'I know that; you don't have to rub it in. But I love you and damn the thing can I do about it.'

'We can't go on like this.'

'Who's complaining? I don't mind sharing.'

I am too fond of her to say what I should, to do what I should. She said, 'Mind me, Cormac, just for tonight; love me even for a little while.'

FOURTEEN

When teaching me the fiddle the master showed me how to do variations on scales, and then demonstrated the rules of harmony. These come in very useful as I polish my birthday present for Ria. My piece of music harmonises E^b and G. Still a few counterpoints to try out in search of the meaning I want to express. My music must tell her how beautiful she really is; must wash away those things in the past. Beethoven's *Romance in F Major* comes to mind. Oh, to be able to compose music with feeling like that!

If I were of Ria's social class she would be lady of my manor. Perhaps that's why I can be so open with her. An attachment like I have to Margaret is out of the question. Yes, I'll have a lady; the question is, which one? But I certainly won't have a manor.

She looks magnificent on my early return from the estate. My bath is ready. Afterwards I change to the clothes laid out on the bed in my office. Even in this quiet wing I am aware of the buzz.

'When are you going to give me my surprise, Cormac?'

'Not now. I'll pick the time.'

'You're teasing me.'

'I know, and I love it.'

'Oh it's wonderful already, Cormac, and it hasn't even started. Thirty we have; imagine thirty people for my ball! Come into the lounge and I'll introduce you. You'll have a drink before dinner, of course?'

I saw her immediately. Joy was engaged in conversation with

the squire, whom out of courtesy I now addressed as Sir Henry, along with General Phillips and his lady. I hadn't seen her since Southampton. She looked less forbidding in a ballgown, like a freshly clipped horse. Still she did nothing to brighten her immediate environment. Halfway through Ria's introductions she charged over to us. 'Cormac, you devil, caught you at last.'

'Did I do something wrong?'

'Look at him! If I had you in Melbourne I'd have horsewhipped you. No of course I wouldn't. But he's a stubborn one, Victoria my dear; he'll take handling, mark my words.'

'Tell me more,' from Ria, with a light in her eyes.

'"Priorities and principles" he calls them. But he's damn useful around the place: ask the general.'

Dressed as I was and introduced variously as the surveyor, and Victoria's friend or escort, and in a position to keep a conversation going among any group because I didn't have to worry about being other than myself, I wasn't regarded as being out of place. I felt at home.

Ria's dress was green, hugging her body to her waist and then flowing out and down to her ankles. An emerald necklace and earrings she had just received from her father were displayed cleverly by the styling of her dark hair. Shoulder length, it was braided at the sides and clasped at the back to complete a beautiful picture.

Sir Henry sat at the head of the table with Ria on his right. I sat on his left with Joy to my left opposite General Phillips. If Dad could see me now! If Brad could see or hear me now!

Dinner is accompanied by the rich aromas of vintage wines, brandy and cigar smoke. I pace myself on a red that has a message for each tastebud. Gifts are formally presented after the squire's speech. Ria mimes to remind me of her present. I shake my head and smile. The drawing-room leads on to the Great Hall, our ballroom for the night. A five-piece band brought in from Killarney provides the music. I tip off the band leader on my plans. He will make the announcement at the end of the first dance, a slow waltz which Ria and I lead.

She moves beautifully. I tell her so. I tell her that the way she looks tonight is bound to attract the man of her dreams, if he has eyes to see. She is about to speak when the leader announces:

'And now, my lords, ladies and gentlemen, your attention while Cormac gives his present to the Lady Debutante.'

I bring a chair to the middle of the floor and seat Ria on it. The leader hands me my fiddle and bow. I go on my left knee before her; the leader announces that I have composed this piece of music specially for the occasion.

The feeling from the night of my first salmon gathers in my stomach. Then I knew I could escape; now there is no way out. Brash promise but I must see it through, for Ria. I remember Brad's advice: 'Gather your mind to what you're at'. I dry my fingers. Ria beams.

I play, looking into her eyes. She is beautiful. Thank God my music is saying what I feel. She closes her eyes, tilting her head slightly back. Her bosom heaves. I reach my crescendo and hold. Ria leans forward, tears in her eyes. She's even more beautiful. She kisses me. We hold each other.

I catch a glimpse of Joy, jubilant as if I had completed a clear round. Squire allows a faint smile as if watching a kill. I hold his eyes until he looks away.

'I will never ever forget this, Cormac. You must play it for me again and again.'

Later in the bed in my office, the cool sheets against my skin, I dwell on the events of a wonderfully happy occasion for Ria. I feel good. My promises to her really came alive. A light knock. She enters, hesitates, moves towards my bed in the moonlight, a dressing gown over her nightdress, and sits on the edge.

'I couldn't sleep; I don't want to sleep, Cormac. I hope you don't mind.'

'No, I'm glad. I was just thinking about you.'

'Me too; thinking about you, I mean.'

There was something about the way she said it, the way her body expressed it that aroused a confusion of feelings for her. I reached out. She came to me.

'I'm going to kiss you, Ria.' She kissed me like before.

'No, Ria. Let me show you, nice and slow, like this.'

In the morning I awake to the happiest debutante in the world snuggled up beside me, and the biggest problems in the world knotting up my insides. I had given her back to her world that first time: now I would have to do it all over again. I am left on my own as I work on my survey to lunchtime; just King Henry, Dozy the pointer, Mazie the red setter, and me. I feel derailed into emotional confusion. Work is my refuge.

The estate needs more trees, more protection from the elements. The meticulous cutting back of its hedges leaves it looking naked and vulnerable, hence the erosion. Shaved nature must now be saved. Ria will own this place soon. The buds of nature must be allowed to germinate for her, more like Lazy Ned Wally's place over yonder, neat but natural where birds can nest in privacy and safety for their young.

Margaret Wally? Betsy Foran? Ria Wallace? Thunder; calm; lightning. If only; if only. If Brad could see inside my head now! If my father could! If my father could?

Highgrove could be renamed 'Happy Manor' at lunchtime. It even seems to have rubbed off on Joy. Ria is different, more confident, no trace of the loneliness which had dulled her eyes. Back in the office I begin to sketch. I can see the estate in my mind's eye the way it should be. Squire has done a great job over the years, gradually taming the upper slopes of Hare Mountain into fertility. Five hundred acres of productive land overlooked by the defiant last few hundred capping Hare Mountain, a mountain that would very quickly reclaim its own if care wasn't taken. Mountain intruding on estate or estate on mountain? Me? Am I secretly in league with that mountain?

Squire enters.

'I need to use this wall opposite the bay window as one of my drawing boards.'

'Feel free; whatever you think best. There are bigger walls on some of the other rooms if you need them.'

'I've never been through the house.'

'I'll get Victoria to show you around. Amazing what people, a bit of life, does for a house like this. Actually that's why I'm here; that gesture last night, your present, seems to have worked wonders for her; most unusual and tasteful.'

'Thanks. I was wondering about your gesture when you rode away from me?'

'I thought you were following.'

'I'm not going to give up on this. I know I'm right.'

'So that makes me wrong?'

'Wrong isn't always the other side of right. What you're clinging on to is not a right, not any more. Have you thought of how that farmer is going to explain the position to his prospective son-in-law?'

'Yes, damn you, I have. I'm still thinking.'

'I'd like to help.'

'Help! Assist me out of my inheritance, so to speak?'

'Think of what it will mean. There's resentment out there. Muffled, inarticulate but it's there. Be generous; you'll be their hero.'

Ria enters. 'I hope I'm not interrupting anything?'

'Actually – is the General downstairs?'

'Yes, Father, they're all waiting for you.'

'As you can see, Cormac has been sketching the estate on to this wall while we've been talking. Hasn't been through the house yet; you might show him around. See you for dinner.'

He was gone, leaving us alone.

Another slow kiss, lingering, confusion boiling. Is it possible that something impossible is happening?

'Thanks for such a wonderful night, Cormac. You didn't mind me sleeping over with you, did you?'

'I didn't wake you. I kissed you and you just purred.'

'Really?' She laughs and observes my work.

'Is this going to be a mural?'

'It could be; meantime it'll be a bit more practical. Your entire estate in one room.'

'This was always my favourite room, the smallest one in the house.'

'And now?'

'It will always be where my life began. Could you do a mural for me, a living piece?'

'After I finish the survey, I'll try.'

'What's the name of my present?'

'Beautiful Ria.'

'Will you play it again for me, please?'

Brad showed me a 1952 entry in Bailiff's diary.

'What's the use! These people are friends in Rex's nose.'

'Let's hope we won't have to do it for much longer.'

'You're not giving up on me just when . . . ?'

'Just when – what, Brad?'

'I want you to be the next *Brad*.'

'But it's supposed to be father to eldest son.'

'Your father gave you to me as an eldest son. Anyway my own, Laurie, couldn't get a fish out of a bucket.'

'I am honoured beyond words. I don't know what to say.'

'Say you'll accept. You've proved yourself.'

'If that's what you really want, yes.' His arms are around me; I try to match his enthusiasm.

Surely this mantle will smother my budding relationship with the daughter of the manor. Already it weighs on my strategy with the squire. Tonight I will have to consummate my title by taking a salmon from the Glens. Brad has done the spotting for me so I know where to go.

'You're very late, Cormac.' She stowed away a ledger.

'Yes, Mother, I know. Delayed longer than I expected.'

'Anyway you asked me to wait up; the kettle is on the boil.'

'A drop of tea would be lovely.'

'No need to ask if you're all right. You've trouble plastered all over your face.'

'I didn't think it was that obvious.'

'Troubles of the heart, maybe?'

'Did you ever have those?'

'Every mother has.'

'Was Brad talking to you?'

'He told me what he planned. Is that what this is about?'

'What do you think? What would my father think?'

'We think you'll do fine.' We supped our tea while I considered my next move.

'Have you spoken to Brad?' she interrupted.

'Oh yes; I told him I'll take it.'

'You know that's not what I asked.' She waited.

'I don't know what's happening. Some things are going great; yet I'm like a drake in a torrent.'

'Work and play, in that order?'

'I wouldn't call it play.'

'Dynamite then?' There was a kindness in her probing.

'How do you know?'

'You're in love with more than one?' I nodded.

'And is your love being returned?'

'Now that you mention it, I'm in debt.'

'That's not so bad. Which one of them would you take on a picnic?'

'Lemonade and homemade buns?'

'I think you'll figure it out all right. Don't fly too close to the flame. Take your time, that's all I'll ask.'

If she only knew. I would have to fly through that flame.

The film in the Ballybo picture house is David Lean's multi-layered comedy *Hobson's Choice* bringing great performances out of Charles Laughton, Brenda de Banzie and John Mills.

'So how did things go at the manor Wednesday night?'

'Very well. Everything turned out fine. How about the rambling house?'

'I couldn't go, could I?'

'Why not?'

'Because you were otherwise engaged, that's why.'

'You shouldn't be depending too much on me. You should have other friends.'

'She has come between us, hasn't she?'

'Betsy?'

'Well?'

'Have you ever been out with anyone else?'

'I don't want to be out with anyone else!'

I feel as if she has kicked me down low. I change the subject to the film. We laugh at Brenda de Banzie's scheming and arrange to meet at the rambling house on Sunday night.

Saturday is hunt day at the manor. Squire asks me to lead out as I know the terrain so well. Brad has given the fox a good start. This lad means business, a golden male that seems to know all the tricks. I have to work at keeping the pack on the real trail. He has thrown down a challenge and must not get away with it. For hours he sets his elaborate pattern of decoy trails before setting off on his diagonal variation to the cliff edge over Owmore river, the place where Ria took her tumble. I summon the entire pack with the horn and get the horses to head him off. In his temporary confusion the pack arrives. The kill is swift and decisive.

I pick him up; a seven-year-old in his prime. He could be the one that worked the same manoeuvre four years ago. I can understand why they enjoy this. Joy is ecstatic. Ria is glowing. The visitors leave on Sunday, taking the fox skin already prepared for the taxidermist.

Monday, Tuesday, Wednesday I press towards conclusion of the survey. I cannot pin the squire down to progress on my other agenda. Ria wants me to stay over another night. Thursday I start on the mural.

I have to finish, tomorrow; returning to London Saturday. Betsy is travelling with me.

'He knows you've been looking for him, Cormac. He says we can talk over dinner tonight.'

'Do you know what we've been talking about, Ria?'

'I've got it out of him, yes.' I worked on and waited.

'I haven't really heard your side of this business.'

I could feel she wanted to hear it, to try to understand, so I took her through the history of the problem right up to my father's death.

'Oh my God, I never realised.'

'That's my side of the case in all its grim reality. And there's something else; it'll be just the three of us for dinner?'

'Yes.'

'I'd like to provide the starter. I'll get it lunchtime.'

'I'm sure it'll be another surprise.'

'Yes. Every bit of it.'

'I'll have a surprise for dinner too, in code. I hope you can decipher it.'

As the visitor, I am invited to say grace. We tuck into the smoked salmon. Squire remarks on the quality.

I hope Ria won't mention the source. She doesn't but gives me the ideal cue when we finish.

'Now, father, isn't that the best you've ever tasted?'

'Excellent, Victoria; excellent actually. Thank you.'

'Don't thank me; thank Cormac.'

How does a man look when he realises he's caught? 'Please take it in the spirit it's given, Sir Henry. In fact under your rules the fish was yours anyway; but under my principles of justice it was mine.'

'In other words you poached it?' Ria's face registers shock, or amazement.

'I took it from the river on Thursday night.'

'You took it? How?'

'That's my secret. I believe you are familiar with the significance of the name *Brad MacRua?*'

'Yes: your uncle, your grandfather . . .'

'And now it has been passed on to me; we've just eaten a portion of my title catch but I don't plan to use the title as a poacher.'

'But you just said you . . . '

'Father! How long more are you going to keep this up? What Cormac is looking for is only common justice; and I think the smoked salmon makes the point very well.'

'Victoria, I'm trying to work out an approach to this problem: spoke to Phillips about it actually.'

'Good; what did he suggest?'

Squire's demeanour suggests unease.

'The General is a practical man, Father. A bit pompous perhaps; but it can't be that bad?'

'He suggested that I refer the matter to – Cormac, not realising he was the one under my skin about the whole damn thing anyway.'

Ria laughs. There is an amusing edge to the irony. Squire does not appreciate it. She teases him, enough to restore his appetite.

'I'll try to find an honourable way for you to deal with this, Squire. I'll write to you during the next few weeks. How's that?'

'General's idea going to your head, is it?'

'No. You'll have a document to work on.' He considers, then offers me his hand. We shake.

'Well done, Father. And now that we're on formalities I want to clear the question of my marriage, in principle.'

'Your marriage! To whom?'

'I cannot say. He hasn't asked me yet. But he is a man, a young man known to you and Major Phillips and I'm in love with him.' Her voice caressed the last few words.

'But I haven't seen you with anybody in ages.'

'That's it, you see. Sometimes we cannot see the obvious, right under our noses.'

'But this chap mightn't know the first thing about running an estate?'

'By golly, he does, and he knows how to get his quarry.'

'Then where was he for your ball, if he's all that wonderful?'

'Father, please! I said I can't tell you because he hasn't asked me, yet; so when he does ask, may I accept?'

'Well, I should be ever so happy for you, but what if he doesn't ask?'

'I believe he will. So please, may I accept, subject to your approval?'

'Well, yes; that's more like it.' We catch the dismay in each other's eyes as he turns to me.

'Can you make anything out of that, Cormac? Women seem to enjoy these riddles?'

'It's a surprise to me too. But I am happy for you, Ria.' She studies my face. I try to hide my heart. I know my chances ended the moment I became Brad MacRua. I force myself to eat. The wine helps. After dinner I go straight back to the mural. I'm doing it in coloured chalk because of lack of time.

My feeling for the job has changed. But I promised to do it. How stupid of me to think that I could be one of them. Me, master of this estate! A poacher, he called me. Tears. Stupid naive me! And still I feel I almost poached her. Yes; it was close, I'm sure, if I had been bolder. But I had been bolder: oh Christ.

I put in the additional trees; more foliage in the hedges, reduce the size of the high fields. She's behind me. I didn't hear her come; my concentration must be off. I continue to work from the stepladder.

'It's very late, Cormac. You will stay, won't you?'

'No, Ria; I can't. I have to get home. I'll finish these high fields and then go.' I stress the word 'go'.

'All right. Good night, Cormac. See you tomorrow.' She lingers.

'Good night, Ria.' I work on. Why am I doing this?

Why has she, whose world I cannot be part of, kicked the legs from under mine? My eyes are heavy. I almost tumble from the ladder. I'll take a nap on the bed and then come back to it.

What's this? A room full of sunlight, a quilt over me, no shoes. The aroma of coffee. Ria enters with a breakfast tray.

'I'm glad you stayed, Cormac. You were out cold when I came back to check, so I covered you, and stayed beside you until you warmed up. I hope you don't mind.'

'Who is he, Ria?' That look of sadness again in her eyes.

'Think about what I said, Cormac. Some things are so obvious, right under our noses, that we cannot see them.'

She looks at me, her eyes tender, pleading. 'I also said I'll wait for – I'm waiting to be asked.'

Fifteen

Back in London I get down to writing the formula to allow the Squire to grant their rights to the smallholders. It cannot be a surrender. He must appear to come out of it as benevolent benefactor. Moreover I must get it done before the new Squire takes Ria's hand.

This adversary has given me an opening I must explore. Margaret and Betsy will wait. Ria is gone anyway, according to her own words, yet each move she made before I left, each tear she shed, the way she held me on my departure spelled contrary signals.

Enough! I can no longer dodge my father's business, impelled by the title handed down to me by Brad.

> Whereas I, Sir William Henry Wallace, Bart., of the Barony of Cnocaceart in the County of Kerry, beneficial owner of Highgrove Manor and all the Lands and Rights vested therein and thereon, in consideration of their friendship and skill in the farming of their lands, hereby bequeath the game and fishing rights over the lands of several smallholders named attached, to these named smallholders:
>
> Provided:

1) The said smallholders shall form Gun, Game and Fishing Club(s) under the Wildlife Preservation and Conservation Rules as amended from time to time:

2) No smallholder shall exclude from his lands or waterways persons duly authorised to exercise bona-fide game and fishing rights under the above rules, save

a) a landowner who has reason that a person or persons abuses these rights and the landowner's rights, said landowner may appeal to the Club Committee.

3) The owner/occupier of Highgrove Manor together with his/her guests from time to time, and particularly on the occasion of the twice yearly hunt shall have specific rights agreed in the rules of the above club.

As signified by the signatures of each smallholder on the one hand, and my signature on the other hand, this document shall execute the formal conveyance of this bequest.

Agreed on this . . . day of . . . nineteen hundred and sixty . . . and given under our hands

_____

William Henry Wallace, Bart.

_____ Witnessed by

_____

_____ Witnessed by

Weekend London is turning into a circus. Crowds congregate in places like Chelsea and Petticoat Lane, market stalls, buyers, browsers, pickpockets, buskers, tattoo artists.

On Sunday mornings conflicting interpretations of the Bible, other books, and governments, are belted out from soapboxes at Hyde Park corner. Garish hats and sunglasses make up for lack of musical talent and taste. But oh, what an escape. It is theatre of the street throbbing on the fringes of life. I develop an act, Ethel Gibbons designs my costume, the veterans buzz: new action, renewed life.

A lampshade converted to a hat with a couple dancing on springs on top, a bedspread rejuvenated as a poncho and kilt, a pair of long green socks I got from Mags-the-well and dancing shoes, attract attention even before I play a note of music. The gramophone horn on my fiddle begs curiosity anyway. The effect is magic.

This is another world, a world to amuse the ordinary citizens, a place where day-to-day worries cannot find a toehold, a means of bringing joy even for a moment into hearts that never smile. Only three weeks gone, three Saturdays in Chelsea and Sundays in Petticoat Lane. My part of the money exceeds £500 with £250 to the home. I can buy a new car for that if I want to.

A new week, an envelope in Ria's handwriting containing an envelope in Squire's handwriting.

Highgrove Manor
15 Sep 1960

Dear Cormac MacRua

You obviously went to a great deal of trouble in preparing that legal document to persuade me to grant your wishes.

I feel however that the interests of Highgrove Manor are not sufficiently well protected and secured. So I am referring the matter back to you to see if you can look after my interests as well as you have secured your side.

Of course the matter has taken a new twist now that Victoria's clues as to the identity of her intended fiancé add up to you. That being the case we all have some further thinking to do.

Your document is returned herewith. No doubt I'll be hearing from you very soon.

Yours truly
W. H. Wallace
Baronet of Cnocaceart

Can this actually be true? Where's Ria's letter?

Highgrove Manor
18/9/60

My dear Cormac

Father has give me his sealed letter to post to you. I'm not sure what he is saying but please understand that he was very impressed with your document, as indeed am I. He has also decoded my message given at dinner that night before you left, and he is probably referring to that. I never dreamed he could be so happy for me.

Cormac, there is something really important I want to discuss with you. It would be unreasonable to expect you to come to me so soon; anyway a visit to my cousins is overdue. I'll be arriving in Euston station Friday, that should be the Friday after you get this. I would love if you could meet me before I travel on to Epping or maybe even travel with me.

Cormac, my love, in case you don't remember me whispering it, I am now telling you again that I love you. The feelings you have stirred in me, the tingle you have brought into my life, the everything about you makes me so happy to be alive, more alive than I could ever have dreamed.

So now you know. We must talk. Until I see you on Friday here's
all my love,
Yours always
Ria X . . .
PS   I think I have memorised all of 'Beautiful Ria'. I'll play it on
cousins' piano for you.
Love, Ria

I feel as if I am being borne up that cliff rising from Owmore
river to Highgrove. I want to grip something, to consider, to
contain my surging joy. Oh God, this is what I want but it is not
what Margaret Wally wants, or Betsy Foran; and most certainly
not Brad MacRua, or rather Brad MacRua, senior. Father? Mother?

Would Ria be the one I would take on that picnic?

Oh yes; and she would have her own homemade scones; and
she would love it.

Father! Have you any idea of how much your fight has become
mine? How it has made me suffer initial sneers that later warmed
to my achievement? How it conspired with the guile of your brother
to make me lust after every audacious move of the poacher? How
it drove me to learn land law just to fight one case?

Now it's our fight, yours and mine; a fight, not only for rights
but for something more personal.

Of course it's impossible, Father, depending on the way you
look at it. The poacher's son winning, not just the gamekeeper's
daughter, oh, Betsy please try to understand, but winning and
marrying the baronet's daughter! The fact that I want it, that she
wants it, doesn't make it right. Discrediting the name of Brad,
making it a laughing stock? Brad will see it that way but that is
not the way it is. What way is it? Ria, a prize for winning a race?
Margaret, resting so snugly in my heart, until now. Oh, Margaret.

'You're dead right, Cormac; relax for a day in the office for a change. You missed this letter, the one from Dublin.' Ethel leaves me to my anxiety.

Dublin

19/9/1960

Dearest Cormac

You're only gone back a few weeks and I'm missing you already, hoping you can get home at Christmas so that we can get together again. If you're not coming home I'm going over there, so please let me know your plans.

Your advice to go into this career is proving right.

I have just been offered my first promotion and I want you to be the first to know. I'm writing this from the office and rushing to catch the post. Please write soon.

Love

Margaret XXXX

PS Sorry about the scene with Betsy after the Rambling House that night. I hope she got over it all right.

Yes, Margaret; she got over it all right but when Betsy gets upset she takes a lot of consoling.

To use John Mills' expression in *Hobson's Choice*: 'My word!' At seven in the morning, Ria's poise and style turn the heads of all who are not blind, in Euston station. We take a taxi to Veterans' Home where Ethel has tidied my office and made a breakfast table out of my desk.

'No mural in this office, Cormac?'

'No reason for one.'

'I'm glad.'

'Is everything all right, with yourself?'

'Fine; perfect. Is this the type of breakfast you like every morning?'

'You didn't travel all this way to ask that.'

Her laugh reminds me of something I've put away.

'I'd never have seen myself in this role, you know.'

'I know.' There was a softness in her lilt.

'What time are you expected in Epping?'

'Sometime this evening. I can telephone ahead.'

'Can it wait until Monday? You can stay here. I want to show you London at its best.'

'Really! A whole weekend together, and today as well?'

'Ethel will connect you later.'

I could feel her observing me; the way she replaced her cup in the saucer heralded a question.

'Problems, Cormac?'

'At all levels; practical and emotional.'

'Emotional?' Her eyebrows arched in surprise.

'I have two other girlfriends and they won't be pleased. One in particular will take it very badly.'

'I'll help you. After all, I caused it.'

Another unexpected aspect of her character.

'How can you help?'

'One of them is Margaret Wally and the other Betsy?'

'Right first time.'

'And Betsy's over here, nursing near Epping?'

'Yes.'

'Then we'll go and meet her; or I can meet her myself.'

'No. This is my problem, Ria.'

'Our problem, Cormac. From now on your problems are mine.' She squeezed my hand, and sealed the deal with a kiss.

'Now the practical problems I think I can make a good shot at.

There's this business with my father that you've nearly solved anyway. By the way, he thinks he owes you more money.'

'No, he paid what we agreed. But there will be a big problem of principle, with Brad.'

She filled her pause by pushing back her chair and walking around behind me. 'But you're "Brad" now, aren't you?'

'Yes, but at his wish. It's a family trust. To marry you, in his eyes, would be the ultimate betrayal. I don't know if I can convince him otherwise.'

'You're very close, you and Brad, aren't you?'

'We've grown together after having had our differences; closer than ever. I don't want to hurt him.'

'I can almost feel it. And your mother?'

'My mother is – my mother. She'll understand, or try to understand, anything I do.'

'That's beautiful; the way you said that. And she'll be my mother-in-law, grandmother to our children. She was the only one could cope with my mother before she died.'

'When are you going back?'

'Oh, they should manage without me for a week or so.'

'I'll have to go back and speak to your father, finalise the rights issue with him, to clear any cloud from our plans. And I have to speak to Margaret Wally.'

'If it's going to be that difficult maybe you should just write; you're very good at finding appropriate words.'

'No! No! No! It can't be true! tell me it's not true, Cormac,' Margaret Wally pleads. I say it without words. Conflicting feelings. I want to hold her, to tell her – what? I watch her agony bursting through her eyes, handkerchief replaced with a towel. How can I do this? My cruelty wringing searing moans of anguish from a heart that loved me. What can I do? The pain of causing this, and doing nothing; helplessness.

She rises, slightly stooped, holds the back of her chair. Margaret Wally. Words cannot express the accusation in her eyes. Anger replaces agony. The anger of realisation, the killer of her emotions lurking here.

'I think you should go.' She looks down over a Dublin street. 'Now, Cormac, please.'

At the door I search for words.

'Cormac?'

I wait.

'No. No; best not.' I can feel the ache of her tension. Disappointment, anger shredding her spirit. No relief, no satisfaction in the thumping lump in my chest. I close the door and tiptoe back through the splinters of her heart.

'Margaret!' Sobs intersperse her gasps.

'Margaret.' I place my hands on her shoulders. All her movements, her breathing, stop.

'Margaret, I can't do it: I can't leave you like this.'

'Sit down.' A compelling authority in her hoarseness. 'You said you love her, that you're about to marry her.'

'But I've just realised how much you . . . '. Realisation chokes my words. She sits in the front half of her chair.

'So where does that leave us?'

She is poised in that chair opposite me, her wet gaze intense. I grope for an answer. Ria floats on my confusion. Where *does* that leave us? My father, the rights I have almost won – where does this leave them?

'Well, Cormac?'

'I'm sorry, Margaret; why can't it be like when we grew into that first kiss!'

She moves behind me, elbows on my shoulders, gentle hands comforting me. 'I love you, Cormac: I want to help.'

We talk.

In the morning she joins me on the train back to Kerry: a moving cage rattling, fractured reality prowling with me through the carriages. She allows me my silences, smalltalking the intervals until we reach Millstreet.

'What do you really want, Cormac?'

'What do I really want? To snip off the tentacles of the squire and his estate that intrude on every smallholder's rights. Yes; that must come first.'

She sinks back in her seat. 'That's ridiculous.'

'From a MacRua point of view I have reneged on other duties of my legacy. But I can deliver this one.'

'Small thanks you'll get for your trouble.'

And still the rhythmic challenge in the rattle of the train. *Brad MacRua, Brad MacRua, fight your battle, Brad MacRua. Cormac Nua, Cormac Nua, shed your baggage, Cormac Nua.* The train slows down over the points pulling into Killarney. *You're on your own; do it. Think now – on your own; do it.*

'You'd better get off, Cormac; we're here.'

'Cormac, what's – ?'

Ria locked in shock. My God, what have I done to one so beautiful! Hurt and fright distort her features, like when I found her clinging to that bush during my first hunt. She flees. Margaret's grip on my arm restrains me.

'She has seen enough to know what's happened.' An air of triumph I cannot identify with in Margaret's voice. 'This way is best, Cormac. The culture gap would only swallow the two of you.'

What she was saying made some sort of sense but the life that struggled with the death inside me rejected it. Ria's anguish, Margaret's triumph, the spoliation of my happiness. And wherefore now my business with Squire?

My bed is too small for me and my labyrinth. I walk the Glens, picking my steps through dense nothingness. Ria, her face at Killarney station, at the manor when she refused to speak to me. Engraved hurt, as when I first touched her in that blackthorn bush: sobbing, moaning pain. Is this what Ria's pillow is witnessing tonight, every night, because of me? Torture: hers, mine. Now I cannot squeeze away her tears with my thumbs.

And if she were to allow me, what of Margaret? I am the foundation of her happiness adrift in my own storm.

I follow a pathway through the forest up to the babbling streams of the Glens. Peace in the familiar sounds, comfort in the scents. I am not alone. Someone nearby in the night.

'Trouble in your bottle, whatever it is.'

'I don't think you can help this time, Brad. There are others involved.'

'That's plain to be seen. You're not the first man had to face things like this.' He waits. I want to talk but don't know where to start. He eases down beside me.

'Things aren't going your way. Maybe you're in too much of a hurry; a step back might help you to see the rabbit.'

'Maybe; but I've multiplied the problem.'

'She has her eye on you, hasn't she?'

'Who?' He knows I know. I wonder how he would react if . . .

'Is that your problem? Have you an eye for her?'

'She hasn't her eye on me any more and she's blocking me from getting at the squire.'

'What about Margaret Wally; isn't she more in your line?'

'What about Margaret? What about what I'm trying to finish?

Plenty backward steps there I assure you! And I was so close.' We walk and talk back through the forest.

'What did he think of whatever was between ye, his daughter and yourself?'

'He seemed pleased. Oh I was within – almost there.'

Mother has obviously been up; the kettle is singing over the fire. Brad makes tea, Mother joins us.

'You were saying about being close. Close to what?'

I explained about the letters, of how things advanced during the survey as my relationship with Ria developed.

'No wonder you're in a mess, your heart ruling your head.'

My heart or my head couldn't argue with that. They observe me. I am sand flowing through a sieve. Brad continues: 'You're going nowhere with a muddle like this clogging up your head. Remember what I always told you, warned you!'

'I know!' I feel sorry that I opened up.

'And these women: has your silly heart made up its mind?'

'I don't know!'

'Christ Almighty!'

'Oh, Cormac! You haven't got – you're not in any trouble, are you, son?'

'Not that kind of trouble, no, Mother.'

'Thank God.'

'The squire won't like this, his daughter falling for you and he in favour. He'll blame you and he'll be right. You didn't promise anything?'

'We agreed to marry but that's all blown away.'

Brad went very pale. I could see him trying to swallow.

'That's your trouble, isn't it, son? Some sort of a deal you had to do to win these rights?' Mother pleaded.

'No; there was no deal; it was on my own terms.'

'You're in a bigger mess than we thought. Many's the man would turn in his grave if you went through with this.'

He blinked and swallowed. "'Tis bad enough being in cahoots with them people, but marrying into them after what they've done to us, turning your back on your dead! No! It won't work.'

'Please, Brad, it's all finished now. She was in love with me and I with her. Remember what you and Mother went through to get married?'

'That was different; no comparison. They killed your father. The bastards killed my brother and my sister and my father. You're dancing on their blood, you treacherous bastard . . . '. Mother sprang to my side.

'Brad MacRua, as God is my judge, I am leaving this house tonight with my children if you don't withdraw that word about my son.'

Silence, suspended on the ticking of the clock, almost cracked. Her grip tightened on my arm. He wavered.

'That word only: everything else stands, and more with it. I'll never have a thing to do with it; never. England and education and high ideas turning him into a traitor under a MacRua roof.'

A mad fire in his eyes. I search for something to say but the tornado in my head has a young boy at its epicentre with Brad MacRua as his hero, the most important man in his world.

My father; dying alone in a stable yard. Father, surely you would understand? Or will you rise out of your box in the dead of night and burn this cloud of shame into my soul from flaming sockets? Hands clutch me; Mother's hands, voice pleading.

'Cormac, you had better go to bed, my son; better say no more for now. Don't lose heart, Cormac, not now. I am proud of you, very proud. You too, Brad. To bed, and no more of this blood rushing.'

He pushed back his chair, gulped what was left of his tea and placed his mug on the table. His last duty each day was to rake the ashes over the embers.

'Ria is a fine young woman when you get to know her,' Mother observed.

'Maybe if he went after what he's supposed to be after it might keep him away from what he's not supposed to be after.' He paused at their bedroom door.

'You know yourself what your trouble is. Go after your prize fish, and don't leave trout be scattering your eyes. And maybe a wink of sleep might rise a bit of sun in your haze.' He went to bed.

'He's right, about your trouble.' She held me.

The Glens
13 October 1960

Dear Sir W. H. Wallace

Thanks for your letter of September 15.

My efforts to reach you in the meantime have failed, mainly due to my upsetting Ria. I regret this; the loss of Ria's friendship has dulled the excitement and wonder of my life. I will try again to convey my feelings to her.

I believe it would be wrong to allow these difficulties to intrude on the important business you and I have nudged to the brink of resolution. I believe I have the formula to meet the spirit of the requirements in your last letter. Please find it attached herewith. In a way my crisis with Ria has brought the resolution into focus.

I'm sure you will agree after studying the attached that, far from appearing to surrender anything, you will come out of this as a benevolent hero.

I have to return to London for about a week and should be back on

Monday. I will take the liberty of calling on you then, and will hope to finalise matters.

Yours truly

Cormac MacRua

The Glens

13 October 1960

Dear Ria

Please allow me to express my regret at the way things between us have shattered.

Obviously I was not ready for the generosity and truth of your love. I'm very sorry that you should be a victim of my confusion and indecision. Regardless of what you think of me, you will always be special to me. If that pain is still gnawing at you, please forget it; I'm not worth it.

I'm off to London for a few days to help Ethel with a problem. I hope to meet your father for what should be our final meeting when I get back. I hope you might also allow me a few minutes then, after which I will not trouble you further.

I am sorry . . .

Cormac

The film in Ballybo is Cecil B. DeMille's *The Ten Commandments*. Charlton Heston, Yul Brynner, Anne Baxter and Edward G. Robinson pull us between good and evil with a little help from God and His elements. Lightning, the parting of the Red Sea, forty years of wandering, and after all that, Moses has to watch Joshua lead his people into the Promised Land. Margaret's head resting on my shoulder, we kiss through the orgy. Her unique scent, her soft firmness.

Ria tugs at my consciousness while I am with Margaret;

Margaret when I think about Ria. On our way home, standing with Margaret at her father's gate, I consider my course of action should the squire renege on my plan.

'Cormac!'

'Yes, Ria; sorry, Margaret?'

'I knew it, I knew it. A wren wouldn't fit into the bit of space you've allowed for me.'

'Margaret, you don't understand.'

'Ah, but I do. I'm not a fool. You should take a look at yourself.'

'This is very important, the core of my life, until it's finished.'

'Cormac, I've been thinking, about things you said, about me having other friends.' I waited.

'Things aren't right between us, Cormac. The fun is gone, and God did we have fun! But this business that killed your father, well 'tis after killing the Cormac I knew.'

'I don't know what to say, Margaret. In a way I suppose you're right.'

'See what I mean; you're all droopy and overloaded.'

I couldn't argue with that.

'I'm doing this because I love you, Cormac. Please try to understand.'

'I don't know what to think.' She held my face in her hands, and kissed me. We kissed and held each other for a long time.

'What are you going to do, Cormac?'

'See this through with the squire, whatever it takes.'

'And Ria, have you heard from her?'

'No.'

'What will you do when you do? Hear from her, I mean?'

'I can't see that happening.'

'Not the way you are at the moment, I suppose. You'd want to be thinking about it though, to be ready.'

'I've a job to finish; until that's delivered I cannot think of anyone.' She stepped back from my agitation.

'I hope you'll be all right: I want you to be happy.'

'Happy! Well, thanks for that, Cormac.'

She kissed me once more, her hand on my cheek. Tears. 'Goodbye, Cormac; be careful.' She cycled into the moonlight.

SIXTEEN

By flying from Shannon I can have an extra day in London and get home on Sunday. Sunday, the twenty-second anniversary of my father's death; no, his murder. Sunday, that special day when I would join Mother on a visit to his grave in Benmore churchyard.

'He was only a fortnight older than you are now when he died, Cormac,' she said as I left for the airport.

I look down on the patterned countryside through breaks in the clouds. Baronies of beauty to the romantic eye, the cruel mockery of Cnocaceart challenging my soul.

Veterans' Home, harbour in the tumult. Ethel lays out the planning problem on my desk for Friday's appeal. 'I suppose I shouldn't ask, but I'm asking anyway: what's wrong, son?'

'What's wrong! Well, I've managed to lose a fiancée and a girlfriend since I saw you last.'

'Couldn't make your mind up or holes in your heart?'

'Right on both.'

She patted my shoulder. 'You'll need a good night's sleep facing into this appeal. Segregating old men and women: God help them and their planning!'

Work. Ethel's intermittent battles with clumsy officialdom. Her Veterans' Home has to expand to meet demand from state services but now they want her to build an eight-foot dividing wall through the grounds to segregate the sexes. The Veterans don't want that. Ethel recognises it for the stupidity it is. I must find engineering flaws and other snags in the planning requirements.

This is a world I know. My footing is sure: nothing for my emotional indecision to mess up. Well after midnight we compare notes. Ethel too has done her work. Her angle should once again highlight another ridiculous aspect. She goes to make a hot punch while I get into bed. We sip and talk. She wants to know everything about my final submission to the squire. Thankfully she enquires no further into my emotional misadventures.

'Good night, son. No hurry in the morning: we're not on till ten.'

I lie back. Strings trickle from her office, the soothing music of Mozart.

On the flight back across the Irish Sea on Sunday morning I wonder if my luck can hold. Victory for Ethel and her residents lingers as I contemplate a possible meeting with Squire tomorrow evening. I wonder if my father is aware of my emotional desolation as I marshal my thoughts for the final MacRua battle with the obduracy of Baronet Sir William Henry Wallace. If everything goes well I think I'll make that trip to Australia. My work at home will be done.

The implications of that last statement dawns as I approach home in the Glens. But something's wrong. Niamh greets me. An envelope from the Manor bearing my name sits on the window-board. While I open it:

'They're all gone to the Manor. Everyone got cards like that last Friday.'

> Sir William Henry Wallace, Bart., cordially requests
> the ~~presence~~ absence of *Cormac MacRua* at Highgrove Manor
> on Sunday next at 3.30 p.m. to hear an announce-
> ment of benefit to all landowners in the barony.

The bastard! He figured I wouldn't be here, and he's running with my plan, taking me at my word. Now he'll be the hero, delivering the promised rights. The card is a decoy to get Mother and Brad on side, the bastard!

'I'm going up there, Niamh; two hours late or not.'

'That's what Mammy and Daddy figured, so hurry on.'

I drive around through the farm entrance and leave my car near the stables. Squire's revenge for Ria on the double. Tiny Carmody steals towards me. 'Aye, young Cormac. A mighty crowd, and all come in by the avenue. A great day.'

He offers me a sup from his bottle. I refuse.

'Is everybody here, Tiny? All the smallholders?'

'The lot. Did you ever think you'd see the day?'

'I had hopes, Tiny; I had hopes.'

'She's looking well herself too after a spell of the sulks. Rode out the King this morning, she did.'

'That's good. Did Squire make a speech?'

'Sure I was only in the kitchen. You should try the punch; 'tis only ojious.'

My father must have fallen for that one, I thought.

I slip in through the east wing, past my office. I can hear the murmur from the Great Hall. Papers on the table outside the door.

'Whereas I, Sir William Henry Wallace, Baronet of Cnocaceart, in consideration of the loyalty and harmony with which you as a smallholder have maintained your relationship with Highgrove Estate, doth hereby grant you on this . . . day of October 1960 . . .'
It continued: my words, verbatim.

So what am I to do now? Barge in there, announce that my agreed words find their place over Squire's signature after my strategic negotiations with him? And what then? What was the purpose of it all, to probate my father's testament, surely? Now the squire has stolen it for his own purposes; revenge for Ria, perhaps. But at least four people know: Squire and Ria, Mother and Brad. Others will have a good idea.

What's the point, what does it matter, once my father's work has been consummated? I must see Brad without being seen, if possible. The Killarney Quintet are playing background music. There'll be no 'Beautiful Ria' tonight. Groups in animated conversation. Ria with Mother and Julie Wally.

Squire leaves Brad and goes through to the drawing room. I find Brad examining a stuffed pheasant.

'I thought you'd never turn up. What kept you?'

'Never mind that now. Has he made his announcement?'

'Not as such. I thought he was waiting for you.'

'So he knows I'm due back today?'

'Didn't I tell him myself, and then he went off in there with a face on him.'

My blood rose for one final encounter.

I stood at the door of his study.

'You're back early.' He was uneasy, like the time he was looking for my father's box.

'Thanks for the card. I gather I'm just in time.'

'I specifically requested you not to come. Do you have any idea of the extent to which you have stripped this estate, made us a laughing stock, not to mention your appalling treatment of my daughter?'

Something happened: triggered reaction. The redness of his usually sallow face, the fire in his eyes, his trembling grip on the document folder. The estate as a victim of my actions? Ridiculous; preposterous, on my father's anniversary. But he still hasn't formally announced the concessions.

'I wrote to Victoria. I hope we can meet and clear up a few things. But I'm not leaving until you earn the adulation I promised by acting on our agreed words.'

'Adulation! Of whom?'

'Don't underestimate them; they're your neighbours. Do this and they'll never let you down.'

'And if I don't?' Could he possibly mean this?

'I don't think you're that stupid.'

'I resent your attitude. I will not be threatened!'

I want to climb over that desk and kick his pomposity in the groin. I want to whack him across the head with a riding crop. Then the supercilious toff might feel threatened. I see him raising his hand; the index finger jabs the inch in front of my face. He bellows: 'Get out of my house. You have no right to come back and coerce me!'

In his wild stare I have become my father. I gamble. 'Brad has a copy of my final draft, the one you copied for your hour of glory.'

'This was supposed to be confidential.'

'Amn't I lucky I didn't take you at your word!'

'How dare you!'

I produce a copy of the document he has prepared.

'Father, Father, what's . . . oh!' Ria flies to his side. I keep my eyes on his.

'In three minutes, Sir William Henry Wallace, Bart., Brad MacRua, Senior, will tear open that envelope and start reading.'

'What's this; what's going on, Father?'

'But if you go out there and open your document, and apologise for the death of my father, then my envelope will remain sealed.'

Ria babbles. It draws his eyes to hers.

'Shut up, Ria!' I yell.

His eyes dart back to mine.

'Brad must be feeling that envelope, Squire!'

'Damn you, MacRua!'

'Do it, Sir.' I look at Ria. 'Get him out there; they've waited long enough.'

I observe from the shadows of the balcony. Ria stands beside him. Hush.

'You are all very welcome, each and every one of you,' Ria announces, 'and thank you for joining us for what should be a great occasion. Pray attention please for my father.'

Applause. His eyes search the hall. He coughs. 'Thank you, Victoria.

'Ladies and gentlemen, landowners. As Victoria said, thank you all for accepting my invitation to – for this historic occasion. Indeed history weighs heavily on the evolution of this day.'

Please, Sir blooming Squire, don't break down now. He collects himself: 'Over the years the MacRua family have suffered in ways connected with this house. I myself was involved in what turned out to be the death of Cormac MacRua, an event that visited me this very day, this very hour. I lost a worthy adversary and a man who could have been my friend. This community lost a natural leader: the MacRua family one of the finest in an exceptionally resolute and gifted line of men. A young woman was deprived of her husband, and a boy yet unborn lost his father.' He struggles: 'May God forgive me.'

He gasps. Oh, Father we must forgive him. I must get down to him. Mother and Brad reassure him as I get there, Mother and Ria embrace. I offer him my hand.

'In the name of my father, I forgive you, Sir.'

He clings on: 'And you, do you forgive me?'

'Yes.'

He grips my answer in both hands, twitches, brightens.

'You're a free man, Sir Henry; share it around.'

More hush.

'I mentioned that I lost a worthy adversary, but the good God in His wisdom inflicted on me, in place of the father, an even more dogged and resolute son.' He pauses. 'A young man aged beyond his years by bitter legacy, young Cormac MacRua . . .' he looks at me. Is that pride I see in his eyes? He continues, ' . . . who left the Glens as a boy and returned as a man to negotiate with me what I am about to read to you.'

Applause.

He starts to read. I blink and swallow. Again he hesitates. Ria offers him a chair. He hands her the document; she passes it to me.

'You read it.'

Afterwards a hug and handshake from Brad meaning words he could not speak. He passes me to Mother.

'They can rest in a proud grave now, Cormac.'

The poise of her demeanour would have made them proud.

Ria goes to the kitchen. People gather around the squire and Brad. I escape into the dusk. It is done.

I walk. Falling leaves leave a starkness in the trees on the avenue. I follow the downward slope of the fields, searching. But what have I lost, or what else have I lost? Myself. The thrust of my life, my reason for living consummated in climax in one day, one evening, one hour.

I find myself at that place where Ria took her tumble, where Aunt Ellen . . . Peace; prayers for each of them in the whispering dusk.

The dyke I recommended in my plan has been dug, the saplings in place along the precipice. I jump across on to the ledge. There's the dusky blackthorn, the drop to the Owmore. What if there hadn't been a blackthorn? What if Ria had . . . ? What am I thinking? What now?

My past has passed. My present? Soft murmur of the river in flood, the breeze whisking the chill of the evening.

The chill of the evening. A Heather Hill night steals around me. Me, night after dawn; the child I produced now romps around the Great Hall; the womb, this place readying itself for new life. I am discharged.

Somewhere back there a horse trots on cobblestones, excitement of dogs, King Henry's trot! Galloping?

Australia. I have so much to learn about life, about getting a shape on heart and emotions. A salmon. I'll take one last cock, stuff it, a symbol to bring with me as a memento of the good things about this place. And I must take Mother on our promised visit.

Dozy and Mazie fuss around me: I'm sure their kennels were closed. Horse and rider follow out of the dusk. King Henry; Ria's voice. It is she. 'Cormac, what do you think you're doing?'

'I was about to ask you the same thing. You shouldn't be riding around here at this hour.'

'I had to find you. The dogs and the King seem to know you better than I do.'

'I wanted to meet you too; I'm glad it's happening like this.' She dismounts.

'I got your letter.'

'I meant what I said; I would never want to hurt you.'

'I'd never have guessed, the way you harassed father and me.' There was no harassment in her voice.

'Did I have a choice?' She hands me the bridle straps.

'You're bold and headstrong but I love you even more, if that's possible.'

She walks off towards the manor. King Henry prompts me to follow. We catch up.

'I think the least you could do after all this is play my song, let the people know what you once thought of me.'

'I still think very highly of you; always will.'

'Until an old girlfriend gets hold of you?'

'I haven't my fiddle with me; didn't think I'd need it.'

'There are plenty available, the quintet, Master O'Donnell, Dandy Reilly.'

'I didn't see the master.'

'He arrived as I started looking for you. He said you'd have to be found before the music started.'

'I'll play; glad to, of course.'

'Thanks. I'm obliged.'

'You're not worried my reappearance might spoil your father's dinner?'

'Your non-appearance might. You don't really understand him, do you?'

'There's a lot I don't understand.'

'Well, if you're not in too much of a hurry . . . '

Sir William Henry Wallace, Bart., of Highgrove Manor, County Kerry is pleased to announce the engagement of his daughter Victoria Mary to Cormac MacRua, Esquire, Dip. Ag. Eng. of the Glens, Killarney, County Kerry.'

Our wedding takes place in Benmore Church. The combined hunts, Ethel and Veterans, Betsy and her nurses join our friends to fill the church. But it remains empty until I hear my family filling the seat behind me. Laurie, my best man, indicates that we should rise. Niamh leads the bridal procession.